BULLET BRAND

BULLET BRAND

BRADFORD SCOTT

WHEELER
CHIVERS

This Large Print edition is published by Wheeler Publishing, Waterville, Maine, USA and by BBC Audiobooks Ltd, Bath, England.
Wheeler Publishing, a part of Gale, Cengage Learning.
Copyright © 1966 by Bradford Scott.
The moral right of the author has been asserted.

LIBRARY OF CONGRESS CATALOGING-IN-PUBLICATION DATA

Scott, Bradford, 1893–1975.
   Bullet brand / by Bradford Scott. — Large print ed.
     p. cm. — (Wheeler Publishing large print western)
   Originally published : Bath : Gunsmoke, 1966.
   ISBN-13: 978-1-59722-970-8 (pbk. : alk. paper)
   ISBN-10: 1-59722-970-9 (pbk. : alk. paper)
   1. Large type books. I. Title.
PS3537.C9265B85 2009
813'.54—dc22   2009002067

BRITISH LIBRARY CATALOGUING-IN-PUBLICATION DATA AVAILABLE

Published in 2009 in the U.S. by arrangement with Golden West Literary Agency.
Published in 2009 in the U.K. by arrangement with Golden West Literary Agency.

U.K. Hardcover: 978 1 408 44182 4 (Chivers Large Print)
U.K. Softcover: 978 1 408 44183 1 (Camden Large Print)

Printed in the United States of America
1 2 3 4 5 6 7 13 12 11 10 09

BULLET BRAND

1

"Well, Shadow," Ranger Walt Slade, named by the Mexican peons of the Rio Grande river villages, *El Halcon* — The Hawk — remarked to his splendid, black horse, "we still have quite a few miles to cover before we reach that town of Gato, so soon as I throw together a small surrounding we'll be on our way. Figure, if things work right, we should make it by mid-afternoon, getting an early start as we are."

However, if *El Halcon* but knew it, "things" were *not* going to work right.

"Gato!" Slade resumed as he began kindling a small fire. "Funny name for a town. *Gato* — Cat. Understand they tied that loco appellation on to it because of the prevalence of mountain lions in the hills, before the cattlemen about cleaned them out. Until a little more than a year back, it consisted of a big general store that serviced the cowmen of the section, and two or three houses.

Then a prospector struck a silver ledge, a big one, in the hills close to the southwest. Now it's a roaring frontier boom town with all the trimmings. Perhaps it will be a permanent pueblo, but perhaps it won't. All depends on how the silver ledges hold up. If the ledges don't, it is but a matter of time until it vanishes as did so many in the mining area of California, and as some have here in the Big Bend country of Texas. People will drift off to fresh pastures, the houses will be torn down, the lumber carted away. Soon only scattered debris will mark what was once a bustling community. It will be forgotten, and a coming generation will not believe it ever existed.

"Change! Change! Always change. Nothing may endure. Men and women, empires and cities, thrones, principalities, and powers. Mountains, rivers, and unfathomed seas, worlds, space, and universes, they come and they go. That is the inexorable law. Time was when these mountains that surround us were level plains. Even now they are weathering down, lessening, their crests lowering, until once again they will be plains; then to the tune of terrestrial convulsions, volcanoes spouting fire, they will rise once more. Geological manifestations prove it has happened many times in the past, and will happen again in the unplumbed future. Nothing may endure. That is, nothing but God, and the soul of man.

"Well, guess I've moralized enough for one spell. Here's a final helping of oats from the pouch. Top them off with a nibble or two of grass and you should make out till we reach town, where, with good luck, we'll find a stall for you, and a bed for me. I could use one for a change."

With which he got busy preparing his own breakfast. He had spent the night under a tree near a trickle of water, with the saddle for a pillow, and before daybreak the ground had become a mite hard. The prospect of a bed was alluring.

Soon the fire was going to his satisfaction, bacon and eggs sizzling in a little skillet, coffee bubbling in a small flat bucket. That, with a hunch of bread, provided a satisfactory meal for a hungry man.

After cleaning the utensils and stowing them in a saddle pouch, Slade cinched up and swung into the saddle.

A gallant man on a gallant horse! The picture was complete. Walt Slade was very tall, more than six feet, with chest and shoulders commensurate with his height. His waist was lean and sinewy, his arms long. His face was in harmony with his splendid form. A rather wide mouth, grin-quirked at the corners, relieved somewhat the tinge of fierceness evinced by the prominent hawk nose above it and the powerful jaw and chin beneath. His hair was thick and crisp, and black as Shadow's glossy midnight coat. That sternly handsome countenance was dominated by long, black-lashed eyes of very pale gray. Cold, reckless eyes that nevertheless always seemed to have little devils of laughter dancing in their clear depths. Devils that could, did occasion warrant, be anything but laughing.

Bibless overalls, soft-blue shirt with vivid neckerchief looped at the throat, well-scuffed half-boots of softly tanned leather, and a broad-brimmed, dimpled "J.B.," the "rainshed" of the plains, were his costume.

Just an unusually neat chuckline riding cowhand with itchy feet and a yen to go places, a casual observer would have said. That was how *El Halcon* wished to appear. An observer less casual would probably have noted with interest the double-cartridge belts circling his waist, from the carefully worked and oiled cut-out holsters of which protruded the plain black butts of heavy guns. They also would have noted that from the butts of those big Colts his slender, muscular hands seemed never far away.

An unusual adjunct to Slade's armament was a long, razor-sharp knife, the haft of which protruded from one boot top. He had taken it from a gentleman who made the mistake of trying to use it on him, and had regretted his rashness via a swollen jaw and a badly sprained wrist. It was a good blade and some Mexican *amigo* would be glad to receive it.

After mounting, Slade paused a moment to appreciate the wild beauty of the scene. The sun was just peeping over the towering crests of the Santiago Mountains and waves of saffron light were flowing down their rugged slopes like bright water. The grasses were blue with wind ripples and a-glint with the myriad jewels of the dew. The inner surfaces of the cottonwood leaves gleamed pale silver, and the crooked branches of the mesquite were tipped with golden flame. Far to the south, the unreal masses of the Chisos — Phantom Mountains, piled upward into the deep blue of the Texas sky, mani-colored, mystic, cloud-like. Red, purple, blue, and yellow, they typified this land of great distances and desolate beauty that promised to the understanding heart contentment and peace.

Slade had crossed the grim barrier of the

Santiagos by way of the pass through Persimmon Gap. After, he turned west by a trifle south, negotiating the slopes without difficulty, and continued into the wild heart of the Big Bend.

The Big Bend! Always a trouble spot, where the outlaw roamed and honest men fought bitter battles to protect their property, and even their lives. This was the third trip *El Halcon* had made into the wastelands in a year.

"Looks like you might as well take permanent residence in the blasted area," Captain Jim McNelty, the famous Commander of the Border Battalion of the Texas Rangers, told his Lieutenant and ace-man when he dispatched him to the forbidding region. "Get one mess cleaned up and another busts loose pronto. 'Pears to be a regular hell raiser of a town south and east of Alpine. The sort of thing that grows up like a toadstool in the dark, and just as pizenous. Sheriff has set up a branch office, with a deputy on duty steady, and spends more time there than he does at the county seat. Just the same it 'pears things are plumb outa control. Okay, go ahead and see what you can do."

After which, Captain Jim, with snorts and growls, turned to his work, confident that before long things *would* be under control. Slade headed for the turbulent Big Bend in a satisfied frame of mind; he had experienced some lively times there and looked forward to more of the same.

All morning, Slade rode steadily westward. About noon, the lush rangeland over which he passed began to thin out, to merge with the bronze-gold desolation of a strip of desert. Far to the south, and out of sight from where he sat his tall horse, was a silver thread in an emerald tapestry, which was the Rio Grande. Beyond loomed the blue and purple and velvety-red mountains of Mexico.

Skirting the rim of the desert, he rode on across the whispering sands, a lonely figure in all the immensity, past gnarled butte and fantastically carved chimney rock of a sinister land with which the hand of time had dealt harshly. He knew he was now no great distance from his destination, the roaring boom town of Gato. The trail he followed showed little sign of travel.

Abruptly he straightened in the saddle. Faint and wavy with distance, sounded the crack of a rifle. Again and again it snapped wickedly, swiftly drawing nearer, an ominous, menacing sound. Slade reached down and made sure his heavy Winchester, a long-range special, was free in the saddle boot. Over the quivering soundboard of the sands drifted a whisper of fast hoofs.

Directly ahead was a long straggle of chaparral, from which the sounds seemed to come, and as Slade gazed, out of the blue and gold of the growth bulged a horseman. He rode drunkenly, swaying and lurching in the saddle, gripping the mane of his fine roan horse. Behind him sounded that ominous crackle of rifle fire.

As Slade gazed with narrowed eyes, into sight surged three more figures. He saw rifles spurt yellowish fire.

"What in blazes, Shadow!" *El Halcon* exclaimed as he pulled to a halt. "Sheriff's posse pursuing an owlhoot? Could be. Fellow's been hit, too, almost ready to drop out of the hull."

The puzzled Ranger stared at the grim tableau. His amazingly keen eyesight could detect no gleam of badge on a shirt front. And the wide-brimmed steeple sombrero, crusted with silver, worn by a huge man who rode a little in front of another almost equally huge, didn't look just right for a Texas peace officer.

Even as Slade hesitated an instant, not completely sure just what was going on, the end came. The roan horse bounded convulsively in the air, his legs shooting out stiffly from his body. They buckled limply under him when he came down and he went end over end like a plugged rabbit. The rider was hurled from the saddle, clear of the trail, and sprawled on the sand, writhing feebly.

The pursuers whooped exultantly and began pouring shots at the prostrate and wounded man. That was too much!

In a ripple of motion, the big Winchester flashed from the saddle boot to *El Halcon's* shoulder; but against the bare chance it might be law officers gone berserk, he held a trifle high as the Winchester belched fire and smoke. Following the booming report, the tall sombrero of the leading rider sailed through the air. Its owner ducked convulsively with a yell of alarm. Again the rifle boomed, and a second hat whisked from the wearer's head. With uncanny skill, Slade cut the third man's bridle in two.

But they were fighters. On they came, yelling and shooting. Bullets stormed about Slade. One plucked at his sleeve like a ghostly hand. He had a vision of faces convulsed with rage. Nowhere did he catch the glint of a sheriff's or deputy's badge. *El Halcon* got down to business.

The Winchester barrel twitched slightly,

15

spurted smoke. The big leader yelped with pain and reeled in his saddle, clutching at a slug-punctured shoulder with reddening fingers. Slade drilled the arm of the second rider and sent a crimson streak leaping across his cheek.

That was enough for the leading pair. They whirled their horses and went thundering back the way they had come, one cursing shrilly, the other, he of the sombrero, reeling and swaying, blood streaming from his wounded shoulder.

But the third man, a lank and scrawny individual, reckless with rage and excitement, rode straight toward that deadly rifle, shooting as he came.

Slade's finger tightened on the trigger. There was a sharp clang of metal striking metal and the rifle spun from his hands. The outlaw whooped with triumph and lined sights.

2

But he failed to reckon with "the fastest gunhand in the whole Southwest." Slade drew and shot, and again.

One of the attacker's glaring eyes went blank. Blood spurted from the ripped socket. The man rose in his stirrups, leaned far back, and pitched sideways to the ground. His snorting horse, reins dangling, flashed past Slade, and came to a halt a little distance off, shivering and blowing.

Slade glanced ahead. The two wounded men had vanished from sight in the brush and he had heard the pound of their horses' irons fading into the distance; he had no fear of them returning. Mechanically he ejected the spent shells from his Colt, replaced them with fresh cartridges, and holstered the weapon. Retrieving his fallen rifle, thankful that the slug which struck the lock had done no serious damage, he thrust it into the boot, and after a single needless glance at the outlaw's body sprawling in the trail, he turned his attention to the wounded fugitive, who was trying to prop himself on a feeble elbow.

He was a middle-aged man with a thin, white face and nervous, waxen hands. His eyes were blue, his mouth firm to the verge of tightness. He was dressed in black corduroy britches stuffed into highly polished black boots, a long black coat, ruffled shirt front, and black, string tie. Blood dripped from the fingers of his left hand. His coat sleeve was drenched with it. There was a slight smudge on the white linen over his left breast.

Slade deftly opened the shirt and glanced at the small blue hole from which a few drops of blood oozed sluggishly. His brows drew together, his lips tightened.

The man struggled onto the elbow of his wounded arm, wincing with pain as he did so. He nodded response to Slade's look.

"Yes, I'm done for," he panted. "Just a matter of minutes."

"Not much blood coming out," Slade voiced comfort he did not feel.

"Bleeding internally," gasped the other. "I can feel myself filling up inside. No, there's no use trying to fool myself. The arm? Just a scratch that doesn't mean anything — now."

He coughed violently and a bloody froth showed on his lips. Slade wiped it away with a handkerchief.

"That's coming from the lungs, arterial blood," the man panted, eyeing the bright red stain. "Time's short."

He seemed to study Slade's face with his slightly cold eyes that were already developing a queer fixed look.

"You're a game one, all right," he breathed. "And you did me a damn fine favor by driving those sidewinders off before they got a chance to slice me into bits or light a fire on me before I cashed in. They'd

18

have done it if they'd got me. That was Red Mike Talco whose shoulder you drilled. He's meaner than a Gila monster. The other two of the same brand. Sure glad you did for one of them. Wish you'd drilled Red Mike dead center, too, for your own sake. He'll be out to even up with you. Don't ever let him get you alive. Got a notion, though, that if he does catch up with you, he won't enjoy what he sees."

"Never mind that," Slade replied. "Lie back and take it easy, now."

The other paid no attention to the advice; he appeared to be thinking hard. Apparently he arrived at a decision.

"Feller," he panted, "you did me a mighty good turn, and I'm going to do something for you, and something for another fine jigger at the same time. You've got the look of a right hombre. Not from this section?"

Slade shook his head.

"Fine! Chuck-line riding cowhand at loose ends, eh? Jerk a thorn loose from that cactus over there, while I get something to write on."

Wonderingly, Slade procured the needle-sharp spine. When he turned back, the wounded man had ripped a square from his white shirt and was smoothing it out with trembling fingers.

19

"Give me the thorn," he mumbled, "and help me keep this rag spread out."

Slade stifled an exclamation as the man dipped the point of the thorn in the blood that dripped from his left hand and began to slowly and painfully form letters on the white cloth.

"What's your name?" he asked thickly, his breath whistling in his blood-filled throat. Slade supplied it and he went on writing, the trembling fingers moving slowly, more slowly. With a last burst of strength, he affixed a signature and sank back against Slade's supporting arm.

"Read," he whispered, gesturing feebly to the red-smeared cloth.

Slade took the fragment and read:

This is my last will. I know what I'm doing, and I'm in my right mind. I'm giving to the man who's carrying this — Walt Slade — my half-interest in my place, the Golconda. Sheriff Chet Traynor, look after this for me.

(Signed) Ralph Marshal

"It isn't just the way the law jiggers would do it, and it isn't strictly legal, there being no witnesses," gulped Marshal, "but folks over to Gato will see things are done like I

20

want them; they think well of me over there. And especially when Chet Traynor okays it. Hunt up Traynor as soon as you get to Gato — fifteen miles to the west — on the trail — can't miss it. A cow town with a new silver strike — plumb salty. Tell Traynor that Red Mike Talco followed me out of town and drygulched me. Tell him what — you — did. Here — take — five hundred — in gold — in poke."

He fumbled a buckskin sack from his pocket and pressed it into Slade's hand.

"Marshal," the Ranger protested gently, "I can't take your money or your property. I have no right to it, and besides, I don't need it. I'll give it to your partner, if you tell me his name."

Marshal struggled against his arm. In his glazing eyes was an infinite pleading.

"Please, feller, do me one more favor," he begged. "Take it and go into business with Black Pete Carter, and lend him a hand. Pete is my partner — he saved my life once, and nigh lost his own doing it. I think a lot of Pete, and he'll need help now. Some folks over there don't go for a — a — for Pete. They put up with him because of me, but he'll have hard going with me gone. Please, feller, will you do it?"

The agonized supplication in the faltering

voice was too much for Walt Slade to resist.

"Yes," he replied, "I will. Don't worry about Pete."

He knew it would make the last minutes easier for the dying man. Also, it would give him an excuse for sticking around Gato, which, conditions and circumstances being what they were, was not to be discounted.

"Don't worry about Pete," he repeated.

Marshal sank back with a deep sigh. In his dying eyes was contentment, and a sudden great peace. He smiled faintly.

"Getting — dark — isn't — it?" he murmured. "And — awful — cold!"

He coughed again, blood foaming over his lips, closed his eyes wearily, and was dead.

Walt Slade stood up, uncovered his black head, and breathed a prayer for the repose of the departed soul.

After, without difficulty, he caught the slain outlaw's horse and draped Marshal's body over the saddle, securing it with his tie rope.

Before mounting, he examined the body of the outlaw. Border scum of the worst sort, was his diagnosis. Cruel, ruthless, not lacking in courage, but behind the door when they were handing out brains.

The man's pockets divulged nothing of significance save quite a bit of money, which he replaced. But the pocket seams interested him. He ran a tentative fingertip up and down the linty surface and surveyed the results.

"May mean nothing, but then again it could," he remarked to Shadow as he swung into the saddle. "Hellion doesn't look like the working sort under any circumstances, although the marks of rope and branding iron on his hands, though faint, denote that one time he was a cowhand. Okay, feller, let's go!"

Although he gave scant thought to Red Mike Talco's possible yen for vengeance, he was alert while passing through the long straggle of brush. Could he have overheard a conversation going on, a little later, in a shack some miles to the south, he would have been mildly interested, and a trifle amused.

Sitting silent in a chair as a companion bathed, padded, and bandaged an ugly bullet furrow in the top of his shoulder, Red Mike Talco did not flinch under his ministrations. His rugged, rather good-looking face was impassive, but his eyes were terrible.

"It ain't bad, Mike," his companion comforted. "High up and no bones busted. You'll be okay in a few days."

Red Mike turned slowly to him and the four other hard-featured men in the shack.

"Run down the big devil who gave it to me," he said, his voice quiet, modulated, but deadly. "When you catch him, bring him to me. Fail up on the chore and I'll have something to say to you, and do."

The others shifted uneasily and turned away from his hard stare.

"I'm scairt he did for Prout," mumbled one, who had a bandage around his arm.

"The fool got exactly what was coming to him," said Talco. "Couldn't he see the big hellion had us totally outranged, and that he's a dead shot? Wonder who and what he is, anyhow."

The others shook their heads. "Seems I've heard of somebody who looks like him and forks a black horse like that," one ventured.

"It doesn't matter," said Red Mike. "Get him!"

Progress with the awkwardly burdened led horse was slow, and sunset was not far off when, from the crest of a rise, Slade sighted the cow and mining town sprawled in the shadow of dark, unlovely hills, like the untidy skirts of a drunken woman. To the north and east of the settlement stretched miles of beautiful rangeland, but the hills to the south and west had a look of stark poverty that was the tattered cloak hiding a vast treasure in silver. Slade had heard that the silver ore had a high gold content, which made it doubly valuable. Above the town hung a shifting cloud of smoke belched from chimneys of its two stamp mills. Long before he reached the ragged outskirts, Slade's keen ears could hear the mutter and rumble of the ponderous iron pestles churning the tough silver ore to a sticky paste from which the precious metal would be extracted by the amalgam process.

Even from the distant rise from which he first viewed it, the town had a vicious and dissolute look, coiled along a spur like a broken-back rattler.

"Tough, all right," Slade said to Shadow. "Old cow town boomed by a metal strike, with all the riffraff of the section, and beyond, swooping down for the kill. Well, those things iron themselves out, sooner or later. The makings of a nice pueblo down there, with decent folks in control and law and order established. We've seen it happen, and will again."

Closer inspection confirmed Slade's initial opinion. Although it wanted an hour of sunset, a sickly glow of lights already showed behind the dusty windowpanes of saloons, restaurants, and stores. Crowds were swirling in the streets, colorful in various costumes. Mexicans in gay serapes rubbed shoulders with brawny miners in blue, yellow, or red shirts. Lithe cowboys strode along with the erect gait of men who spent their lives in the saddle. Here and there an Indian with sullen mutinous eyes slid through the throng as though greased, clad in fringed buckskins, high boot-moccasins, and dingy white turban. Voices rose in raucous argument. Laughter shrilled over the swinging doors of the saloons where boots were thumping and high heels clicking. Somebody was bellowing a song, or what apparently was intended for one.

Stares, sudden silences, and remarks occurred as he passed along the main street with his grimly burdened led horse. But there was that in his stern face and cold eyes that forbade questioning. A crowd quickly followed his progress, at a discreet distance. He approached a young Mexican who was crossing the street, caught his eye, and beckoned. The Mexican turned courteously, took a step forward. Abruptly he halted, staring. Then his sombrero swept the ground as he bowed low.

"El Halcon!" he murmured. "The good, the just, the compassionate, the friend of the lowly. *El Dios,* guard him!"

26

"Gracias, amigo," Slade replied, his eyes suddenly all warmth and kindness. "Can you direct me to the sheriff's office?"

"I will lead you, *Capitan,*" was the quick answer. "I have been there —" he grinned. "The calaboose is in the same building."

In front of the office, Slade dismounted, dropping the split reins to the ground, all that was needed to keep Shadow right where he was until called for.

"Don't touch him," he warned the crowd, that was drawing closer. "Liable to lose half an arm if you do."

The big black was a one-man horse who allowed nobody to lay a hand on him without his master's permission.

Entering the office, Slade found a cheerful-looking, moon-faced individual with a big nickel badge that proclaimed him a deputy sheriff pinned to his sagging vest. He stared at the tall figure confronting him.

"Come outside, I have something to show you," Slade said.

Wonderingly, the deputy followed him, reached the board sidewalk, and rocked back on his heels, his eyes bulging.

"What — what — who —" he stuttered.

"Take a look," Slade told him and gently raised the dead face.

The deputy gulped, his mouth hanging

open. He closed it with a snap.

"Good God! it's Ralph Marshal!" he gasped, turning a menacing eye on Slade and dropping a hand to his gun butt.

"Feller, it looks to me like you've got some explaining to do," he said harshly. "How do I know you didn't kill him?"

"You don't know," Slade answered. "But if I did, it would of course be the logical thing for me to do, pack his body to your office."

Under the sarcasm in the Rangers musical voice, the deputy flushed and looked foolish.

"Guess I sorta talked outa turn," he admitted. "Who did kill him, do you know?"

Slade countered with a question of his own:

"Is Sheriff Traynor around?"

"Oughta be here any minute," replied the deputy. "Ambled over to the Golconda. That's — was Ralph Marshal's place. Here he comes now!"

A big and broad-shouldered elderly gent was shoving his way through the chattering crowd. Suddenly he halted as had the young Mexican, and stared.

"Well, I'll be hanged!" he exploded. "Slade! Why the devil aren't you in jail?"

"Because I'm out," the Ranger replied

28

composedly. "How are you, Chet?"

"Jail," repeated the bewildered deputy. "Say, what in blazes!"

"Don't you know him?" countered Traynor. "Don't you recognize *El Halcon,* the notorious outlaw too smart to get caught?"

"By gosh, you're right," said the deputy, gazing, almost in awe, at the man whose exploits, some of them considered questionable, in certain quarters, were fast becoming legend throughout the Southwest, and elsewhere.

"Aw, Chet, what you tryin' to hand me?" he added in injured tones. "Mr. Slade ain't it? I remember, too, of hearing he was Sheriff Tom Crane's special deputy, up at Sanderson, about a year back. Tom Crane don't take up with no owlhoots."

"Guess you're right," the sheriff agreed.

"But wait," said the deputy. "He brought in a body!"

"Of course he did," said Traynor, glancing at the stark form draped across the led horse's saddle. "He always does; wouldn't look natural without one. Who is it, do you know?"

The deputy's reply was to cross to the body and gently raise the dead face.

"Ralph Marshal!" exclaimed the sheriff, his features setting like stone. "As fine a feller as ever spit on the soil. Bring him inside, bring him inside, and then, Walt, you can tell me about it."

Slade slipped the tie rope loose, cradled Marshal's body in his arms, and bore it into the office, where he placed it on a couch and folded the waxen hands on the breast.

Traynor gestured to a chair. "Squat, and tell me how he come to get killed," he said. "And what blankety-blank sidewinder did for him."

Slade sat down, rolled a cigarette with the slim fingers of his left hand, and recounted his experience on the trail.

"And you figure the one whose shoulder you drilled was Red Mike Talco?"

"That's what Marshal said," Slade answered. "A big man with red hair and blue eyes."

"That was him, all right, the blankety-blank hyderphobia skunk," Traynor growled. He turned to the deputy.

"Hustle over to the Golconda and fetch Black Pete," he ordered. "Chances are he's already heard about what happened. Bring him pronto."

"Red Mike Talco," Traynor repeated. "He —"

"We'll discuss him later," Slade inter-

30

rupted. "First I want to show you something."

He produced Ralph Marshal's "will" and handed it to the sheriff, who read it and whistled through his teeth.

"Looks sorta like you're in the saloon business," he observed.

"I could hardly do otherwise than accede to the last request of a dying man," Slade replied.

"Anyhow, it will sure be a help to Black Pete," said the sheriff. "Here he comes now."

The moment Pete stepped into the office, Slade understood why Ralph Marshal was fearful that Pete would be beset by difficulties. He was a giant of a man, and black as the ace of spades, with brown eyes keen as a falcon's. He nodded to Slade and the sheriff and walked slowly across the room to gaze at the strangely composed face of the man who had been his benefactor and his friend. Slow tears coursed down his black cheeks.

Walt Slade arose and laid a comforting arm across the big man's shoulders.

"He died happy, Pete," he said, his deep voice all music. "He died happy and content. He wasn't afraid to take the Big Jump, and his last thoughts were of you."

"And I'll wager you told him he needn't

worry about Pete," the sheriff put in heavily.

"I did," Slade admitted.

"And he believed you," said Traynor. "No wonder he died happy. Pete, you've suffered a loss, as all of us have, but you're getting a break, too. Sit down, I have something I want you to see."

He passed Marshal's will to the big Negro. Pete read it, handed it back.

"Yes, I am," he said slowly. "And I feel sure we'll make a go of it, together."

"We will," Slade said. "Especially after we've belted some sense into a few loco heads."

"And, gents, he's sure good at beltin'," chuckled the sheriff.

The deputy laughed, and even Pete smiled wanly. Immediately, however, his brow wrinkled and his fine eyes took on a worried look.

"But I'm bothered about you, sir," he said. "Red Mike Talco is liable to come looking for you."

"Hope so," Slade replied carelessly. "That would simplify matters, for I certainly don't know where to look for him."

The sheriff chuckled again. Being "looked for" by outlaws was nothing new to *El Halcon*. Sometimes they even caught up with him, to their grief. Traynor was convinced

32

that soon Red Mike would be one of that forgotten number.

Slade pressed Marshal's rawhide poke into Pete's hand.

"Five hundred dollars, in gold, I believe he said," he remarked. "I didn't count it."

Black Pete didn't count it, either. With a word of thanks, he thrust the poke into his pocket, unopened.

"And now suppose we mosey over to the Golconda for a snort and a surrounding," suggested the sheriff. "Pete can sorta line you up on things, Walt. Chumley," he told the deputy, "you stay here and keep an eye on poor Marshal."

Together they walked down the street to pause before a building with plate glass windows. Over the door was a wooden sign that read:

THE GOLCONDA
Carter and Marshal

3

The Golconda proved to be a big place, well lighted, excellently appointed. There was a long and gleaming bar, the backbar pyramided with bottles, a lunch counter, tables for leisurely diners, others for games, two roulette wheels, a faro bank, a dance floor, and a really good Mexican orchestra. The girls on the floor were young and pretty and, Slade thought, gave the appearance of being squareshooters. Everything was spotlessly clean. All of which, Black Pete pointed out with pride.

"A good holding," Slade said. "Should do well, and even better as time goes on."

"I hope so," Pete replied. "I feel it is my duty to make a success of the business, in deference to Mr. Marshal's wishes."

While they talked, it became apparent that a crowd was gathering in the street outside the building. There was some laughter, rude jests. Evidently the news of the death of Marshal had gotten around.

But it seemed to Slade there was evinced a sinister undertone that was disquieting. Abruptly he turned to the sheriff.

"Suppose we go out and you can introduce me to the folks," be suggested.

"Guess we could do worse," Traynor agreed. "Come on."

A sudden silence fell as he and Slade appeared in the doorway. Traynor looked the crowd over, his grizzled brows drawing together a little.

"Boys," he shouted, "want you to meet the new half-owner of the Golconda, Mr.

34

Walt Slade." A buzz of conversation ran through the gathering.

"Well," suddenly yelled a big cowhand in the front rank, who had evidently looked upon the wine when it was red and various other colors, "Well, reckon that sign up there will have to be changed. I'll make a start."

He jerked a gun from its holster and commenced blazing away at the front of the building, the muzzle tipped up.

"She's changed," he chortled, ejecting the spent shells.

It was. Marshal's name was almost obliterated by splintered wood. The crowd roared with laughter.

Before the uproar died down, Slade had crossed the street with lithe strides. The cowboy shrank a little under *El Halcon's* icy eyes beating hard against his face, but he tried to keep up a nonchalant appearance.

"W-what do you think about it?" he mumbled.

"I think," Slade replied, "that it wasn't a nice thing to do, but seeing as you've started it, I suppose I might as well finish it."

His hands flashed down and up. Both guns let go with a rattling crash. Another moment and he was ejecting the spent shells and replacing them with fresh cartridges.

The astounded crowd stared at the sign, which now read:

"Carter and" — neatly done in bullet holes — *"Slade!"*

The big cowhand let out a whoop that broke the silence. "Gents," he bawled joyously, "that's shootin'! I don't care who he is, what he is, or where he came from, any man who can shoot like that is the bully boy with a glass eye for my money!" The crowd bellowed approval.

"Mr. Slade," the hand added apologetically, "I didn't mean to be ornery. Guess I'm just sorta terrapin-brained when I've had a few snorts."

"Everyone to his own sense of humor," Slade replied carelessly, running his eyes over the crowd, and not unfavorably impressed by what he saw.

Suddenly he smiled, the flashing white smile of *El Halcon* the men, and women, found irrestible.

"And now suppose you all come in for a drink, on the house," he suggested.

It was an offer that such a gathering would be slow to refuse. They streamed into the Golconda, the bartenders got busy. After the free drink was downed, they remained to buy more, to play the games, and occupy the lunch counters and the dance floor. Slade noted, pleasurably, that several men shook hands with Black Pete and sympathized with him over his loss. And incidentally, congratulate him on his acquisition of a new partner.

"You've got 'em," chuckled Sheriff Traynor. "How you do it I don't know. You just grin, and they amble after you like little wooly lambs."

"They're not bad, just thoughtless," Slade replied. "Go ahead and order us something to eat while I go around with Pete and meet the help."

Swampers, waiters, dealers, bartenders, and kitchen help responded to Slade's smile and kindly words. The orchestra, all Mexicans, bowed low, the leader twinkling his black eyes in an anticipatory manner. The dance-floor girls were frankly more than a little interested. Everybody was friendly, with one exception.

The exception was Crane Hodges, the head dealer, a big, bristle-haired man with truculent eyes, who officiated at the high-stakes poker game at the corner table. His reply to Slade's greeting was a surly grunt.

"Crane is sorta put out and on the prod, I'm afraid," Black Pete confided. "You see, he hoped to get in on the ownership of the Golconda. He tried to buy me out, but I wouldn't sell. Mr. Marshal wouldn't sell him his holdings because of me; but Hodges figured that sooner or later Mr. Marshal would pull out and he'd get his chance. Marshal was a gambler first off, with itchy feet, and Hodges knew he'd eventually move on. Now Hodges figures he's lost his chance."

"I see," Slade said, and regarded Crane Hodges with interest.

Sheriff Traynor let out a beller. "Come on and eat," he called. "Chuck's on the table."

After a satisfying meal and a cigarette, Slade rejoined Black Pete at the far end of the bar. A little later, Crane Hodges turned in his chair and glanced expectantly at Pete.

"Mr. Marshal always used to spell Hodges at the table about this time, so he could take off an hour to eat," Pete explained. "I can't handle cards or I'd take over. Can you?"

"Reckon I can take a whirl at it," Slade replied, and strode over to the table.

The moment Walt Slade picked up the deck, the players realized the new owner knew his business. They had another example of it a few minutes later.

One of the players, a young cowhand who really had no business in such a high-stakes game, lost a big pot and laid down his cards.

"Reckon that cleans me, fellers," he said ruefully, and rose to go.

"Wait," Slade said. He shoved a stack of chips across the table.

"A first-class game always stakes the player to a stack when he's cleaned," he remarked. "See if you can get your money back." A murmur of approval went around the table. The cowboy gratefully accepted the offer and immediately began to win.

Some time later, Crane Hodges returned to the table and dropped into a vacant chair.

"My hour ain't up," he said in his surly voice. "Believe I'll try a hand or two myself."

"Open game," Slade replied, without looking up.

The game went on and a big pot built up. After a spirited round of betting, Slade picked up the deck and held it ready.

"How many on the draw, folks?' he asked.

When the turn came to him, Crane Hodges eyed his cards a moment and discarded.

"I'll take two," he growled, laying one bronzed hand flat on the table top.

Slade flipped the two cards to him. Hodges reached for them with one hand and started to lift the other from the table. Something flashed a streak of flame through the lamplight.

"Hell and blazes!"

Hodges' startled yell flickered the hanging lamps. Between his slightly spread fingers, razor-keen edge grazing the flesh, quivered a long knife, its point driven deep in the table top. And every man present knew it could just as easily have been plunged through Hodges' hand, or through his throat, for that matter.

Instinctively Hodges jerked his hand back. Pinned to the table by the knife that sliced its edge was a single card.

"Hodges," Slade said, his clear voice carrying to all parts of the room, "this is a straight game, and palming an ace doesn't go, even to just show up the dealer."

As he spoke, without effort, he drew the knife from the wood and flipped over the sliced card with the point. It was the ace of diamonds.

The players stared. A menacing growl ran around the table and spread over the room. Fierce eyes turned on Crane Hodges, who flushed red, turned white, and didn't know which way to look.

Slade stood up, smiling. He handed a fresh deck to Hodges, who took it mechanically.

"Reckon your hour is about up, Hodges,

and I've got other things to do," he said. "You'd better go on with the deal."

Crane Hodges stared at him, jaw sagging. The other players stared, too.

"You — you mean you trust me to go on dealing?" Hodges asked in a thick, incredulous voice.

"Of course," Slade replied. "Why not? Guess all of us have a loco spell now and then. I don't think you'll have another one soon. Get on with the deal. Okay, Pete?"

Black Pete smiled and nodded, and twinkled his eyes at the stupefied dealer. Slade joined him at the end of the bar.

There was a dead silence at the poker table. Crane Hodges dealt a few hands, in a jerky, mechanical fashion. Suddenly he threw down the deck, surged to his feet and stalked to the bar, face flushed and distorted, eyes glaring. He whirled to face the silent crowd.

"Gents," he boomed, "did you ever see a skunk? You're looking at one right now. But a skunk ain't so bad after somebody slices off his smell bag. Me, I don't figure to smell any more." He jerked his thumb toward the end of the bar. "And over there," he added, "stand the two *whitest* men who ever coiled twine in this blasted section. Anybody who 'lows different will please step close, so I can get my paws around his blankety-blank neck!"

Nobody accepted the invitation. Instead, the room rocked with laughter and hand-clapping. Crane Hodges walked back to the table and resumed dealing as if nothing had happened.

Sheriff Traynor, who had immediately occupied a strategic position when it looked like trouble might cut loose, chuckled aloud.

"I don't think you'll have any more trouble with Hodges," he predicted.

"He's all right, just needed a jolt to straighten him out," Slade replied.

"And he sure got it," Traynor said, still chuckling. "You scared the daylights out him with that sticker. I've a notion he's still feeling sorta queezy around the throat. Wonder why he did that fool thing?"

"Just a stupid little scheme to prove my inadequacy as a dealer," Slade explained. "He was all set to show the other players how easy it was to palm an ace with me dealing. Didn't work."

"It sure didn't," snorted Traynor. "Now what?"

"First thing, I wish to find quarters for my horse," Slade said. "He's been standing outside long enough; time he was made comfortable."

"Come on," said Traynor, "I'll take you to the stable where I pen my cayuse, just around the corner. An old Mexican runs it, and runs it right, with the aid of a sawed-off ten-gauge shotgun. Let's go."

The stable proved satisfactory. The Mexican keeper bowed low to *El Halcon* and exclaimed over Shadow, to whom he was properly introduced, and led the big black to a stall for a rubdown and a surrounding of oats, his favorite provender. Slade shouldered his saddle pouches, leaving his rifle in the care of the keeper.

"And next," he said, as he and Traynor walked back to the Golconda, "is a place where I can pound my ear."

"Pete has some rooms over the saloon that he rents out to folks he figures he can trust," replied the sheriff. "I sleep up there when I'm in town. He'll take care of you. Rooms are clean, and no bugs, which is more than you can say for most of the fleabags they call rooming houses and hotels."

Pete readily agreed to do so and conducted Slade upstairs to a comfortably furnished room second on the right from the head of the stairs, where the ranger deposited his pouches.

"Will be plenty of hot water for shaving

43

and washing," Pete said. "Hope you'll sleep well."

"I'm sure I will," Slade assured him. Together they descended to the saloon, where business was booming.

Knowing it was the thing to do, Slade circulated among the customers, engaging them in conversation. He talked with several ranch owners who discussed range matters with him. One or two mentioned certain difficulties that were confronting them. Slade listened, then advanced some advice which was well received.

"Guess you young fellers with your book-larnin' sorta have the edge on us old codgers," one admitted.

"Not being so busy as you gentlemen, it's just that we have more time to familiarize ourselves with modern methods," Slade replied.

"That's lettin' us down easy," the oldtimer chuckled. "Much obliged, son, for what you told me; I'll follow up."

A really astonished man, however, was the manager of the section's biggest silver mine. Before he realized it, he was discussing his affairs with *El Halcon* in highly technical terms. He mentioned a problem of drainage that had been giving him endless trouble. Slade listened intently, asked a number of questions, which the manager answered.

"Just a minute, sir," the Ranger said. He drew a notebook and pencil from his pocket and drew a diagram. Figures and symbols flowed beneath his slender fingers. An equation took form, and its solution. Slade studied the result a few moments, asked a couple more questions, and changed the diagram slightly.

"There you are, sir," he said, passing the inscribed paper to the bewildered manager. "That should take care of your difficulty. Follow the diagram and the notations and you can't go wrong."

The manager studied the diagram and the figures, his lips moving as he read. His brows drew together and he read them over aloud, as if doubting his own voice.

"Now why in blazes didn't I think of that?" he demanded in querulous tones. "Well, I didn't. Mr. Slade, I believe it will work."

"It will work," Slade stated positively. "I encountered a somewhat similar condition once before."

"And straightened it out, I'll wager," declared the manager, carefully folding the paper and stowing it in his pocket. Slade smiled and did not deny the obvious fact.

"And I'm very, very much obliged to you,"

the manager added. "I'd take it kind if you'd manage to drop down to the mine in the next day or two and make sure we're following instructions properly."

"I'll do that," Slade promised.

"And if you sorta get fed up with the liquor business, after a while, I can certainly use a man like you," the official said.

"Thank you, sir," Slade replied, but did not commit himself. With a nod and a smile, he moved on to speak with others, leaving the manager gazing after him and shaking his head.

Sheriff Traynor comfortably ensconced at a table with his pipe and a snort waved a beckoning hand.

"Take a load off your feet and let's gab a while," he said as Slade drew near. "See you've taken Dick Gord in tow. He runs the Contention Mine, and owns quite a hunk of it. He's a big jigger in the section, and has connections over east, I've heard."

"Appears to be an able and very affable person," Slade commented.

"Uh-huh, whatever that means," the sheriff agreed.

Meanwhile, Slade was being discussed by Manager Gord and the cattlemen and others.

"There are folks who say he's an owlhoot," somebody observed. The remark was received with scornful laughter.

"Well, no matter what else he is or isn't, there's one thing he is," declared Gord. "He dresses like a cowhand, and looks like something out of a story book, but I'll borrow money to bet he's one of the best engineers that ever rode across Texas.

"He has the ability of the really great engineer to look beneath the surface and correctly visualize what's there."

4

The manager wasn't too far off. Shortly before the death of his father, after business reverses that cost the elder Slade his ranch, young Walt had graduated, with high honors, from a noted college of engineering. He had intended to take a post-graduate course in special subjects to round out his education and better fit him for the profession he planned to make his life's work.

That, however, became financially impossible for the time being. So he turned a receptive ear when Captain Jim McNelty, with whom he had worked some during summer vacations, suggested he sign up with the Rangers for a while and pursue his studies in spare time. Long since he had gotten more from private study than he could have hoped for from the post-grad and had received attractive offers of employment from prominent members of the financial and business world he had contacted in the course of Ranger activities.

But meanwhile, Ranger work had gotten a strong hold on him, providing as it did so many opportunities to help the deserving, right wrongs, and bring law and order to sections that before his appearance had little enough of both.

Also, he found happiness in his work, the happiness that comes only from selfless service in behalf of others. An engineer? Yes, later. There was no hurry; he was young. He'd stick with the Rangers for the present.

Anent the *El Halcon* myth — because of his habit of working under cover as much as possible and often not revealing his Ranger connections, he had built up a singular double-barreled reputation. Those, like Sheriff Traynor, who knew the truth maintained he was not only the most fearless but the ablest of the illustrious body of law-enforcement officers. While others, who knew him only as *El Halcon,* with killings to his credit, declared he was just an owlhoot too smart to get caught, so far, but who would sooner or later get his comeuppance.

However, Slade had defenders as well as detractors among those who knew him only as *El Halcon,* who insisted vigorously that he was on the side of law and order and that peace officers of impeccable standing were glad to have *El Halcon* lend a hand when the going got rough, and that he had never killed anybody who didn't have a killing long overdue.

The deception worried Captain McNelty, who was fearful lest some over-zealous marshal or deputy do his ace-man harm. To say nothing of a professional gunslinger hoping to enhance his notoriety by downing *El Halcon,* the fastest gunhand in the whole Southwest, and not above taking undue advantage to attain his objective.

But Slade would point out that as *El Halcon* he was able to learn things a known Ranger could not hope to learn, and that outlaws thinking him one of their own brand sometimes got careless, to their sorrow.

Captain Jim would grumble, but not specifically forbid the deception, and Slade would laugh, and go his careless way as *El Halcon,* satisfied with the present and giving scant thought to the future.

And the Mexican peons and other humble folk would say:

"El Halcon! the good, the just, the compassionate, the friend of the lowly. *El Dios,* guard him!"

And Walt Slade felt he could aspire to no higher accolade.

Sheriff Traynor suddenly chuckled, and shot Slade an amused look.

"See Pete and the orchestra leader have got their heads together and are looking this way," he remarked. "I've a notion I know what that means. Believe that leader and his bunch were at Sanderson when you were there, right?"

"Yes, I think they were," Slade conceded smilingly. "Wasn't particularly surprised to see them here; they hop about from place to place like fleas on a hot skillet."

"Uh-huh, and here they come, and the leader's packin' a guitar," said Traynor, with another chuckle. "You might as well get set."

The leader was indeed making his way through the crowd brandishing the guitar like a war club to clear the path, Black Pete at his heels. Slade had recognized him the moment he laid eyes on him, and of course the recognition had been mutual. However, the leader, a Yaqui-Mexican knife man, had given no hint until he was sure Slade had no objections to being pointed out as *El Halcon;* the same went for his musicians.

50

Reaching the table, he bowed low to Slade, and held out the guitar in an insinuating manner.

"Please, *Capitan,* you will sing for us?" he asked.

"Well, I suppose somebody has to thin this crowd out if we're ever to get any sleep, and I reckon it might as well be me," Slade conceded.

The leader smiled and chuckled, appreciating the joke, and relinquished the guitar.

Conversation died to a hum as they crossed the room together. Black Pete, smiling and nodding and looking expectant, returned to the end of the bar.

On the little raised platform, the leader held up his hand.

"*Señoritas* and *señors,*" he called, "*Capitan* will sing!"

There was a clapping of hands, then silence. Slade smiled at his audience, ran his fingers over the strings with a master's touch, flung back his head, and sang. He knew the gathering, like many another he had faced. So first he sang a song the cowhands loved, a song of the range and the wastelands, the hills and the valleys, the blue ripple of the grassheads bending to the breeze, the gold of the sunshine, the silver of the stars, the bellow of the storm, and the lashing of the rain riding on the wings of the wind.

And as his great baritone-bass pealed and thundered through the room, all activities ceased and men stood entranced.

The music ended with a crash of chords and was followed by a tumult of applause, and shouts for another.

In deference to the many miners present, he sang of the men who toiled in the dark depths of earth heart, with the mountain glooming above them, and Death grinning from behind every dubious supporting pillar.

Turning inward the dance floor, he sang an exquisitely beautiful love song of old *Mejico,* during which the girls gazed upon the tall singer as at a vision from another world, and let the tears flow unashamed.

Turning again, slowly, to where Black Pete stood, he sang, gently, softly, but with every word clear to his listeners, the immortal lines, set to a musical composition of his own, of the poet of the poor:

"Then let us pray that come it may —
As Come it will for a' that —
When man to man, the world, o'er,
Shall brothers be for a' that!"

There was a subdued earnestness to the applause that followed that was a greater tribute to the singer than the burst of sound that had gone before.

Smiling at Black Pete, who bowed his head, Slade returned the guitar to its owner, at the same time slipping the long knife into his hand.

"A good blade, *amigo,* and has served its turn," he said.

"And treasure I will *El Halcon's* gift," the leader murmured, bowing low.

"Is there anything he can't do?" sighed Mr. Gord, the manager of Contention Mine. While from the crowd a voice whooped:

"The singinest man in the whole dad-blasted Southwest!"

"And with the fastest gunhand," chimed in another.

"Right on both counts," declared a third.

"And," said a fourth, "a man to ride the river with!"

When Slade resumed his seat, the sheriff said, "Walt, if you'd promise to sing every night, you'd keep this place filled to the ears."

"Oh, they'd grow tired of it after a while," Slade returned lightly.

"Never!" declared Traynor. "Never!"

And the orchestra leader said to his men, "*Ai!* he sings as sang the Angels of the Heavenly Host, but, brothers, I have noted that when he sings, some evil one will weep!"

Slade beckoned Pete to have a final cup of coffee and a cigarette with him. After which he announced, "I'm going to bed. Been a long and hard day and night, and I didn't sleep too well last night. Be seeing you tomorrow. You, too, Chet."

In his room, he locked the door, drew the window shade and cleaned and oiled his guns. Placing them ready to hand, he tumbled into bed and was almost instantly asleep.

And far to the southeast, four hard-faced men rode purposefully toward the dark smoke cloud blotting the stars, that hung like a hand of doom over Gato.

5

When Slade awoke, sunlight was peeping around the edges of the blind, and from the angle of the rays he knew it was past mid-morning.

While he was moving about, he heard a tap on the door. Opening it, revealed an old Mexican swamper with a tin tub and a huge pail of steaming water.

"For Capitan's convenience," he said bowing low.

"All your roomers receive such considerate attention?" Slade asked, smilingly.

The swamper also smiled. "For *El Halcon,* all," he replied, and departed.

After enjoying a good clean-up and a shave, and donning a clean shirt and overalls, Slade descended to the saloon in search of some breakfast, where he found Sheriff Traynor and Deputy Chumley already at table.

"Figured to try and get an early start and pick up that carcass you left on the trail, if the coyotes haven't beat us to it," the sheriff explained.

"A good notion," Slade agreed. "I'll ride with you."

"Think it's necessary?" said Traynor.

"Could be,' Slade answered. "Chet, just who and what is Red Mike Talco?"

The sheriff shrugged. "Don't know who he is, but he's a reg'lation Border bandit working the same old system," Traynor replied. "Tells the folks along the Border south of the Rio Grande that he is part Mexican and a *liberator* who aims to right their wrongs and bring them justice. You know the sort. Maybe he is part Mexican, I wouldn't know."

"He could be, but I rather doubt it, after getting a pretty good look at him," Slade said thoughtfully. "Of course there have been red-haired, blue-eyed Mexicans, of pure Spanish descent. Juan Flores, who was something in the nature of a real *liberator,* was one; Cheno Cartinas, the Border raider, another. But usually skin coloring and features correspond; Talco has neither. I think about the only thing Mexican about him was the steeple sombrero I shot off his head."

"Chances are you're right, per usual," conceded Traynor. "Anyhow, he's an infernal pest and mean as a striped snake. A robber, a cow thief, a killer, and he's got a bunch of the worst sort following him. *Liberator!* he's about as much a *liberator* as a horned toad. Apologizing to the toad, who don't do anybody any harm."

"The *liberator* is quite popular all along the Border right now," Slade commented. "No doubt about it, the country down there is cruelly misgoverned, and there have been people on this side of the Rio Grande who have taken advantage of conditions to advance their own selfish aims, with natural resentment developing against all Texans, the vast majority of whom do not deserve it. Well, we'll see. Soon as we finish eating, we'll mosey. Okay?"

"Right," agreed Traynor.

Very shortly, they set out, Chumley leading a pack mule that would bear the body of the dead outlaw.

"Should make it back by dark," predicted the sheriff. "That is, if nothing busts loose; never be sure as to that, in this blankety-blank section."

As they rode, at a good pace, Slade constantly studied the back trail, his gaze probing the blue distances his companions' eyes could not penetrate, and as he gazed, his own marvelously keen eyes seemed to grow even paler and colder than was their wont. However, he said nothing to the others until they were within a couple of miles of the long straggle of brush through which the trail wound for more than a mile. Then he announced:

"We're wearing a tail, have been ever since we left town. Four of the devils."

Traynor shot a startled glance over his shoulder. "I can't see anything," he said. "Oh, well, I won't argue with you; those blasted eyes of yours see what nobody else can."

"They don't aim to close in on us until we enter the stand of chaparral ahead,"

Slade explained. "They can't spot us, except now and then, but they know we must keep to the trail, and they can figure all the time just about how far ahead we are. Once they are sure we've entered the brush, they'll speed up, hoping to catch us at a disadvantage while we are loading the body. Must have been keeping watch on us in town, and of course had no difficulty divining where we were headed when we left Gato."

"What are we going to do about it?" the sheriff asked anxiously.

"As soon as we enter the growth we'll speed up a bit," Slade said. "Keep right on going until we are close to the far end of the stand. Then we'll hole up in the brush and wait for them. With good luck, we should thin out *amigo* Talco's bunch a little. If we can manage to take one alive, we may be able to persuade him to do a mite of talking to save his own neck. Might give us a lead to where Talco hangs out."

"If I get my paws on him, he'll talk, and be glad of the chance," the sheriff promised ominously. "Let's go!"

At the beginning of the chaparral, Slade glanced back a last time. Yes, there were the pursuers, mere shadowy blurs against the horizon. He sensed that they had quickened their pace. Closing in for the kill!

Once invisible in the growth, Slade spoke to Shadow and led the way at top speed along the winding trail. Finally he called a halt, just beyond the apex of a bend.

"Okay, into the brush," he ordered. "All right, this is far enough," he added a moment later. "Critters should be safe here; hope they'll keep quiet. Now back to the edge of the growth; I'll hear them coming in plenty of time. You do the talking, Chet. We're law-enforcement officers and must give them a chance to surrender. If they don't, and I don't think they will, shoot fast and shoot straight. It's a desperate bunch and we mustn't let them get the drop on us. Quiet, now, everybody, and let me listen."

Very shortly, his keen ears caught the muffled beat of slow hoofs on the thick dust of the trail.

"All right, get set," he whispered. "They're right at the bend; step out when I give the word."

Another moment and the four outlaws eased into view at the bend, sitting their horses in attitudes of listening, peering ahead to where their expected victims would be absorbed in the task of loading the body onto the pack mule.

"Now!" Slade snapped. The posse surged

from the growth. Sheriff Traynor's voice roared:

"Elevate! You're covered! In the name of the law!"

A storm of startled exclamations arose. The outlaws jerked their horses to a halt and went for their guns. The posse instantly opened fire and the growth quivered to the stormblast of the reports.

But the outlaws were men of grim courage. Taken by surprise and at a disadvantage, they nevertheless fought viciously. Back and forth gushed the orange flashes. A saddle was emptied as both Slade's Colts spurted flame and smoke, and another. He heard a curse behind him and knew somebody had caught it. A slug grazed the back of his own hand. Another ripped his sleeve, barely graining the flesh of his arm. He squeezed both triggers and a third killer spun from the saddle.

With reckless daring, the remaining owl-hoot drove his spurs home and charged straight into the blaze of the posse's guns. Slade shot to wound, not to kill, for he earnestly desired to take the fellow alive.

But the others took no chances and the outlaw fell, riddled by bullets, his snorting horse almost on top of the posse.

"Well, guess that puts everything under

control," Slade observed as he reloaded. "Anybody hurt?"

Deputy Chumley, swearing profusely, was swabbing at a bullet-gashed cheek. The sheriff had a red streak burned along the side of his neck. Slade's left hand oozed a few drops of blood.

"Not bad," the Ranger said, "but just the same it was darn good shooting on their part, caught off balance as they were. A hard and efficient bunch; looks like we've got our work cut out for us, rounding them up."

A pad and a couple of strips of plaster took care of Chumley's cheek. The other wounds were too trifling to bother with.

Next the bodies were examined, the sheriff confiscating quite a bit of money, but their pockets disclosing nothing else of importance. Nor did the pocket seams interest Slade, as had those of the dead man who lay in the trail beyond the growth.

"Mean-looking hellions," was Traynor's comment on their appearance.

"And more intelligent appearing than the average of Border scum," Slade said. "A clever and original scheme that was concocted. Talco or somebody has brains and knows how to use them."

"And if it wasn't for your eyes, the blankety-blank scheme would have worked and we'd have gotten mowed down," growled Traynor.

"Possibly," Slade admitted. "However, it didn't, and that's all that really counts. Well, let's amble out and see if our other specimen is where I left him."

The horses and the mule were retrieved from the brush, the outlaw mounts, docile beasts, easily caught. The bodies of their late unlamented riders roped to the saddle.

As Slade expected, the body of the victim of the previous day's battle was right where he had left it.

"And the coyotes didn't take a chance on pizenin' themselves, either," said the sheriff. "Well, reckon we might as well load him up and then head for town. Going to be a mite later getting in than I expected, but just the same I figure we did a darn good afternoon's work. Quite a collection we've got to put on exhibition. A pity Talco himself ain't one of 'em. I've a notion maybe he's layin low till that hole in his shoulder heals up. Hope it gets pizened and cashes him in. Oh, well, I figure it's just a matter of time till he catches himself a nice little dose of lead pizenin', or finds himself kicking on nothing and sorta short of breath. Either one will be plumb satisfactory from my way of thinking."

Chumley was nosing around the edge of

the trail. "Here's his hat," he announced. "Bob blowed into a stob and hung there. Quite a rainshed."

"In the nature of a trade mark, I'd say," Slade remarked.

Chumley fingered the bullet hole in the crown. "A pity you didn't hold a few inches lower," he said.

"If I'd known for sure what it was all about, I would have," Slade said. "As it was, I didn't know for sure just what the angle was, until they began shooting at Marshal on the ground. Hard to be sure of the right or wrong of a grudge fight, which it appeared to be, and there was just the chance I might be throwing lead at a law enforcement officer's posse. So when I drilled Talco's shoulder, I still held a mite high." Chumley nodded his understanding.

"If you don't mind, I'll keep the darn thing as a souvenir," he said.

"Go to it," Slade told him. Chumley chuckled, and stuffed the silver-encrusted sombrero in his saddle pouch.

"Let's go," said the sheriff. "I'm getting hungry."

The awkwardly laden horses rendered the going slow and the sun had set when they reached the cow and mining town. The excitement created the day before by Slade's arrival with Ralph Marshal's body was nothing compared to that aroused by the grim cavalcade threading its way through Gato's crowded streets to the sheriff's office. Soon a shouting, jostling, questioning throng streamed after the lead horses.

"Quiet!" Traynor roared. "We'll tell you later. Okay, if you're so darn curious, suppose some of you work dodgers lend a hand unpacking these carcasses and shoving them into the office. Get a move on!"

The order was quickly obeyed, the bodies laid out on the floor. The office was jammed to suffocation.

"Sheriff," somebody pleaded. "Won't you please tell us where you got 'em, and how?"

Occupying his chair and hauling out his pipe, the sheriff proceeded to do so, and the part played by Slade was emphasized. Admiring glances rested on *El Halcon,* and men insisted on shaking hands, showering him with compliments.

"And you figure they were some of Talco's hellions, Sheriff?" a voice asked.

"I don't figure anything else," replied Traynor, puffing hard on his pipe.

"And I got his hat," crowed Chumley, brandishing the much-crumpled steeple sombrero. "Slade shot it off yesterday. A pity his blasted head ain't in it!"

A roar of laughter greeted the sally, and somebody shouted,

"Will be next time."

6

Slade managed to change the subject. "Suppose you fellows give them a once-over and see if you can recall anything concerning them," he suggested, gesturing to the bodies.

The crowd peered close; there was a general shaking of heads. However, a couple of bartenders present felt pretty sure they had some time or other served one or more of the owlhoots, but were vague as to where and when or who might have been their associates. Slade turned to the sheriff.

"Is Mr. Gord of the Contention Mine a regular visitor to the Golconda?" he asked.

"Should be there shortly, eating his dinner," Traynor replied. "He's a bachelor and usually puts away his evening meal at the Golconda.

"And that reminds me," he added, standing up, " 'bout time we were corralling a surrounding. All right, you jiggers, outside; I'm hungry. Come back later. Outside! Outside!"

The horses and the mule were cared for

and the three peace officers headed for the Golconda.

"You want to see Gord?" the sheriff asked Slade.

"Yes," the Ranger replied. "Want to have a little talk with him, after he takes a look at the body of the one I did for yesterday."

The sheriff shot him a questioning look, but *El Halcon* did not elaborate, for the present.

The Golconda was already jam-packed, and the slaying of the outlaws was the prime topic of conversation. Slade was again praised and congratulated, and it was some time before they were allowed to eat their meal in peace.

"Gord just came in," the sheriff suddenly remarked. "I'll see if I can get him over here to eat with us."

He managed to attract the manager's attention and invited him to take a load off his feet and feed his tapeworm. Gord accepted and occupied a chair. The sheriff proceeded to regale him with an account of the brush with the outlaws. Gord listened with absorbed interest, and when the tale was finished shook hands with *El Halcon.*

"Congratulations, Mr. Slade," he said. "You've done more in thirty-six hours to frustrate those miscreants than anybody else has in a couple of months. Congratulations!"

"Thank you, sir," Slade replied. "Guess I sort of got the breaks."

"I have another name for it," Gord said dryly. Said the sheriff, "Let us eat."

They had a pleasant and leisurely dinner together. Slade called Pete to have a drink with them. He and Mr. Gord started talking together and discovered they were originally from the same county in Virginia and had a number of mutual acquaintances. Soon they were deep in a conversation that continued until the head bartender let out a beller for more stock and Pete had to hurry to the back room to supply his lack.

After a snort all around and a final cup of coffee for Slade, he said to the manager, "Mr. Gord, would you walk over to the sheriff's office for a few minutes?"

"You wish me to view those bodies?" asked the manager.

"I do," Slade returned.

"Be glad to," Gord said. "Let's go."

At the office, he peered at the dead faces, uttered an exclamation, and pointed to the member of the trio responsible for Ralph Marshal's death.

"I recall that one very well," he said. "He worked in the mill for a couple of weeks.

Was a good worker and knew quite a bit about the business. But was uncommunicative and didn't mix much with the other boys. I suppose that was before he became connected with Talco and his band."

"To the contrary, I am of the opinion he was very definitely connected with the Talco bunch at that time," Slade said grimly.

"But why was he working in the mill?"

Slade countered with a question of his own. "Mr. Gord, I suppose that at times there is considerable money in your office safe, right?"

"Why, yes," Gord answered. "Often quite large sums, especially just before we pay off the mine and mill workers." Abruptly he looked startled.

"You mean they might try to rob the mill safe?"

"I consider it within the realm of the possible," Slade replied. "I think that fellow was planted in the mill to learn the layout, and conditions, and to gain information he would relay to his master, Red Mike Talco. When is your next payday?"

"Next Tuesday," the manager answered. "A week from today."

"Yes, this is Tuesday," Slade remarked thoughtfully. "Well, we'll see."

"You've got me worried," Gord said. "In

68

the course of the attempt, if it should happen, some of my boys might well be killed."

"Dick, I don't think you have a thing to worry about," the sheriff cheerfully reassured him. "Just leave it to Slade. Walt, how in blazes did you catch on that devil worked in the mill?"

"Because of the rock dust in his pocket seams, which he could hardly have collected elsewhere than in the mill or the mine," Slade explained. The sheriff shook his head.

"Is there anything you don't see?" he snorted.

"Plenty," Slade smiled, "but that was fairly obvious."

"Uh-huh, to your eyes! And you really think the hellions might make a try for the money in that safe."

"I do," Slade replied.

"But Mr. Slade," Gord protested, "we work a night shift continually passing to and fro and the office door always open?"

Slade thought a moment. "I suppose the men eat sometime during the night?"

"Yes, they do" Gord admitted.

"And where do they eat?"

"We have a cook shanty that cares for the night shift; the men eat there."

"And for that period the mill is deserted or nearly so?" Slade asked.

"It is," Gord admitted again. "We shut down the stamps then. But it is a very short period, only half an hour. They certainly couldn't open the safe in such a brief period."

Slade smiled slightly. "I understand the mill is but a short walk from here, so suppose we amble over there for a few minutes?" he suggested.

"Certainly," Gord agreed. "Let's go."

The great stamp mill was a scene of hectic activity when they reached it, but Slade, to whom the workings of a mill were nothing new, paid the scene scant attention. Following Gord into the office, he closed the door and without preamble squatted in front of the safe, laid his ear against the door, and began slowly turning the combination knob.

A minute passed, perhaps half of another. He seized the handle, turned it, and the door swung open!

"See?" he said, closing the door and smiling at Gord.

"But how in blazes did you do it?" demanded the astounded manager.

"Quite simple," Slade replied. "Good ears can hear the sound of the tumblers when the combination numbers are passed over. Then just figure the sequence, and there you are."

Abruptly, his face grew stern. "Mr. Gord," he said, "I'll wager that Mike Talco or one of his men can open that old box as quickly as I did. We are getting a different type of criminal in the West, Mr. Gord. He's bringing big-city methods with him. Just as ruthless and deadly as the old brush popper, but with more brains and more know-how. I'm firmly convinced that Mike Talco is of that type. Being able to outshoot the owlhoot is no longer enough for the peace officer; he has to outthink him also."

"Just like you do," chuckled the sheriff. The manager looked dazed.

"Well, Mr. Slade, after this exhibition I'm arguing nothing with you," he said. "I don't know what the devil to do. I suppose the scoundrels will manage to circumvent anything I do."

"I told you what to do a little while ago," Traynor repeated his previous advice. "Just leave it to Walt, and don't worry."

"And I'm going to do just that," Gord declared. "Come on, let's go get a drink. I feel I need one."

At the busy Golconda, that want was quickly cared for, and Mr. Gord developed a cheerful mood. Abruptly he chuckled.

"Was just thinking about what's going to happen to Red Mike Talco," he explained.

"Hope I can somehow be there to see it."

"Perhaps you will be, if it happens," Slade returned smilingly.

"Oh, it'll happen, all right, no doubt in my mind as to that," Gord declared. "Waiter!"

Three quiet days followed. Then suddenly business picked up, at least for Walt Slade.

A girl rode into town. She was a rather small girl with astonishingly big and darkly blue eyes. Her hair was reddish brown, her sweetly turned lips very red. She had a straight little nose, the bridge delicately powdered with a few freckles, her complexion creamily tanned. Her figure left nothing to be desired.

A regulation sixgun swung at her hip, and there was a rifle in the saddle boot. And she knew how to handle both. Her horse was a splendid red-sorrel, almost as fine a cayuse as Slade's Shadow, but not quite.

Asking directions, she quickly located the sheriff's office, dismounted, and entered to find Traynor alone, sitting at his desk and smoking his pipe. He hopped to his feet with a welcoming smile.

"Well, Mary Merril, so you made it," he chuckled. "Figured you wouldn't waste any time after I sent you word he was here. You sure made good time; quite a ride from

72

Sanderson."

"Oh, not so bad," she replied, dropping into a chair and tossing her broad-brimmed "J.B." onto the desk. "And it's partly in the nature of a business trip. You know, I'm in the carting business with Uncle John and Mr. Arista, and I figure we should be able to do some business here."

"Uh-huh, you'll do some business here, all right," Traynor predicted, shaking his grizzled thatch at her in mock disapproval. "Just wait till Walt claps eyes on you! He'll go out like a light."

"I hope I don't find him — occupied," Mary giggled.

"He ain't," the sheriff replied cheerfully. "At least he wasn't. Be sorta different from now on. Oh, to be fifty again!"

"Shut up?" she told him. "You're getting younger every day and more apt with your outlandish witticisms. But I'm starved, and I'll want accommodations for Rojo, my horse — he's starved, too — and a place to sleep for myself."

"I'll look after your horse, and I guess Walt will let you have a room over his saloon," Traynor replied.

"His saloon!" she exclaimed, the big eyes widening.

"Uh-huh, he's in the saloon business, now

73

half-owner of the big Golconda down across the street."

"Heavenly days!" she exploded. "What will he get into next! But you can tell me about it while we eat. The saloon business! Where is he?"

"Over at the Contention Mine stamp mill, talking with Dick Gord, the manager; they sort of hit it off together."

"Oh, he takes everybody in tow," she said resignedly.

"Guess you ought to know," Traynor said cheerfully. "Come on, we'll take care of the cayuse first."

Rojo was duly ensconced in a comfortable stall next to Shadow's and promised the best of care.

"Fetch my saddle pouches," Mary told Traynor.

"They're sure stuffed," he remarked as he shouldered them.

"Well, you can't expect a girl to come calling on a young man without a few clothes," she retorted.

"Hummm!" said the sheriff. "My, but you have a pretty color today; your cheeks are like a rose bush in full bloom."

"Oh, shut up, will you!" she scolded, the roses blooming even brighter.

7

As they neared the Golconda, Mary's gaze fixed on Slade's name on the signboard, neatly done in bullet holes.

"He did that," she stated.

"Uh-huh, a smart aleck shot holes in Marshal's name — he was the former co-owner — and Walt did him one better."

"Always violence," she sighed. "What became of Marshal?"

"Tell you all about it while we eat," said Traynor. "First let's get you organized with a room. Black Pete, the other owner, will take care of you."

Black Pete did, with inherent courtesy. "The very best in the house for her," he said. "Second on the left from the head of the stairs. Come along, Ma'am, and I'll show you."

"Second on the *left*," remarked the sheriff. "Hmmm!"

Mary shot him a disdainful look, and asked no questions.

Black Pete shouldered her pouches and conducted her up the stairs, where he deposited them in the comfortably furnished room.

"I think I'll freshen up a little, but I'll be down shortly," she told him. "Thank you, very much, for everything."

"I am honored," said Black Pete, with a bow.

When she descended the stairs a little later and joined Traynor at a table, she said, "I like him. He's a natural-born gentleman."

"Yes, he's all of that," agreed Traynor. "Never was a finer feller. Walt thinks a lot of him, and he don't go wrong, not even where women are concerned."

"*Gracias,*" she answered demurely. "Hope you're right."

While they ate, Traynor briefed her on Slade's activities. She shook her curly head.

"Always somebody trying to kill him," she said gloomily.

"Uh-huh, but he don't kill easy," Traynor reassured her. "I predict he'll watch a goose walk across all our graves."

"Flat-footed ignoramous," said Mary. "I mean the goose, not Walt. He isn't flat-footed, at least."

"Really, *I* wouldn't know," the sheriff replied innocently. Mary gritted her teeth at him, and changed the subject.

A little later, he chuckled, "Here comes the young galoot, now; this is going to be good."

It was. Slade halted, stared unbelievingly, and strode to the table.

"Mary!" he exclaimed. "How did you get here, and what in blazes are you doing here?"

"Eating," she replied composedly. "Didn't I warn you that if you neglected me, I'd come looking for you?"

"I don't neglect you," he protested. "I always show up, sooner or later, don't I? And I do have to work."

"Oh, I try to take that into account," she answered airily. "That and your various commitments do keep you rather busy. How is she? Or 'shes' I suppose is more fitting."

Slade refused to rise to that jibe. Instead, he leaned over and kissed her, their lips clinging.

"That's better," she said. "Glad you have one to spare. Sit down, dear, and join us, won't you?"

With as much dignity as he could muster, which at the moment wasn't much, he occupied a chair. Mary laughed gayly.

"You look just as you did when I stepped out of the bushes up top Echo Canyon, where I'd been holed up all the time," she said. "You came very near to shooting me. I'd been so entranced by your singing that I forgot to announce myself. It was such a beautiful song."

"And the sort of voice you don't often

77

hear," interpolated the sheriff.

"I was sort of flabbergasted, thinking you had slipped up the slope without me seeing or hearing you," Slade said.

"Which I couldn't possibly have done," she replied. "And then you saved me from Covelo's raiders at the risk of your own life."

"And your courage and your knowledge of the hills saved us both," he added.

"Perhaps," she conceded. "Well, aren't you glad to see me?"

"Of course I am," he assured her. "I suppose Chet is responsible for you being here?"

"Well, I did have a wire sent from Alpine, letting her know you were here," Traynor admitted. "Figured it was the right thing to do. Chumley took care of the chore when he rode to town to see if everything was under control at the office."

"Fortunately I was in Sanderson when the wire came, and not out on the spread," Mary explained. "I sifted sand right away."

"Quite a ride you took, and you sure made good time," Slade commented.

"Oh, not bad, with Rojo," she said. "You know I'm at home in the saddle."

"And — elsewhere," the sheriff observed, and was rewarded for his innuendo with a sniff.

"What you been doing all afternoon?" he asked Slade.

"I was talking with Gord, and looking things over, a stamp mill being interesting," Slade replied evasively.

Traynor shot him a glance, but asked no more questions, sensing that *El Halcon* was not in a mood to discuss the matter further. He'd talk when he was ready, and not before.

Slade called Pete over to have a drink with them and asked a few questions about the business.

"Have another," he advised. "You'd better while you've got a chance; looks like another big night."

Pete smiled broadly, his teeth flashing white and even as Slade's own.

"Since Mr. Slade took over, business has just about doubled," he explained. Mary crinkled her eyes at him.

"He takes everybody over," she said. "How he does it, I don't know. Sympathy, I suppose, or animal magnetism, or youthful vitality or something. At times I've been conscious of it myself."

The sheriff shook with laughter, but kept his thoughts to himself.

Mary jumped to her feet. "Come on, Walt, I'm not hungry any more, so let's take a walk," she said. "I want to watch the sunset."

"Okay," Slade agreed. "I'll be back shortly," he called to Pete.

Sheriff Traynor, fortified with a full glass and his pipe, smiled benignly as they passed through the swinging doors.

On the crowded street, admiring glances favored the tall Ranger and the pretty girl with her arm looped through his. Slade received quite a few salutations from passersby.

"Seems everybody knows you," Mary commented.

"Oh, it doesn't take long for a saloonkeeper to get acquainted," he returned lightly. "Usually the best-known person in town."

"Well, I guess you've been most everything at one time or another, but this is certainly a new departure," she said. "A —" she glanced around, made sure nobody was within hearing distance, "A Texas Ranger running a saloon."

"To such base uses do we come," he replied smilingly. "And to tell the truth, I rather like it. Hope you don't mind."

"I wouldn't mind anything that would keep you permanently in one place," she declared energetically.

"I'll think it over," he promised.

But even as he spoke, his steady eyes seemed to look into far distances, the ever-advancing curve of the horizon, the wild beauty of the wastelands, and — the trail!

Mary sighed and did not pursue the conversation.

Another moment, however, and she had shaken off her somber mood and was her normal vivacious self.

"I like this town," she said. "It's gay, boisterous, lively. Sanderson isn't exactly tame, but it's stodgy in comparison."

"Perhaps a trifle too lively at times," he returned. "After dark, she'll really howl, especially after the redeye begins getting in its licks."

"As I've said before, I guess I'm just a hoyden at heart," she laughed gaily. "For I adore such nights, as you well know. Oh, what a lovely view!"

They had reached the outskirts of the town and stood gazing at the scarlet and gold splendor of the sunset. The mountain crests glittered in the level light, their mighty shoulders swathed in royal purple. In canyon and gorge, the shadows were already curdling. In the distance, the desert was molten silver with an edging of pale saffron, and in the western sky, braving the sun flame, a single great star glowed and trembled. Mary quoted softly from one of his songs:

"Land of the wings of morning,
Land of the bloom of the day,
Cupped in the hand of eternity,
A rainbowed roundelay!"

"Yes, it is that," she said, "Color, beauty, music frozen into stone! Who could keep from loving it!"

Until the exquisite blending of many hues dimmed to steel gray, the lovely blue dusk sifted down from the hills, and the roses of the sky bloomed in silver, they stood silent, then slowly retraced their steps to Gato's teeming streets.

When they reached the Golconda, they found Dick Gord, the Contention Mine manager, keeping the sheriff company at a table. He was introduced to Mary, and after some general conversation, she broached the subject of a carting line from Alpine to Sanderson.

Gord was immediately interested, listening intently as she outlined the plan she had formed.

"I've a notion it would greatly expedite our supply shipments," he said. "Yes, I think you have something, Miss Merril, and I intend to give it serious thought. Suppose you drop in at my office and perhaps we can outline the details and come to some sort of an agreement."

Mary promised to do so.

"You see?" she said to Slade, after Gord departed. "I'm a darn good business woman. Guess it's a gift."

"Oh, sure," said the sheriff. "Roll those big blue eyes and even a hard-shell old bachelor like Gord throws in his hand."

"I didn't roll 'em!" she denied indignantly. "Did I, Walt?"

"Really I wouldn't know," he replied. "They appear to be habitually swiveling.'

Mary glared at him. "I've a notion to walk out on both of you," she declared. "One is as bad as the other. I should have gone with Mr. Gord. I'm sure he doesn't accuse a girl of things of which she's not guilty."

"Neither do we," Slade remarked, pointedly.

Mary thought that one over and decided to pass it up.

"Anyhow, Mr. Slade, from the way this place is packing them in, you have a gold mine here," she said.

"I am only the trustee for those who come after me," Slade replied.

"Yes, I guess that's so," she conceded.

83

"Well, I don't believe I'd have it otherwise; I can't see you cooped up in such a place, nice though it is. Better the wind and the stars and the dust of Gypsy feet, and — the trail."

8

Now the Golconda was really filling up and the crowd, Slade thought, was more boisterous than usual. It was the kind of night when anything could happen, and often did. He became more alert, studying faces, listening to scraps of conversation his keen ears could catch. And not a man came through the swinging doors that he did not note. After a while, he rose to his feet.

"Be seeing you in a little while," he told Mary. "Going to pass the time of day with my customers, and have a word with Pete. Sure we'll dance when I come back; I won't be gone long."

With which he sauntered around the room, pausing from time to time to speak to occupants of the tables, and men at the bar. When he passed the big poker game where Crane Hodges dealt, Hodges nodded and grinned in friendly fashion.

Working his way to the kitchen, Slade sat down to have a cup of coffee with the old

Mexican cook.

"Pedro," he asked, "what do you know of Mike Talco?"

The cook rolled his eyes skyward, and answered in his precise, mission-taught English:

"An evil man of evil companions. Cruel because from cruelty he pleasure gets. He speaks to the ignorant of liberty and justice, but the only liberty he desires is liberty to murder and rob. Justice to him is but a word without meaning."

"Has he many followers south of the Rio Grande?"

"Quite some few among the ignorant and stupid," Pedro replied. "The people have known much wrong and turn to one who promises redress."

Slade nodded. It was an old story along the Border, and sometimes productive of evil, such as the raid by Cheno Cartinas on the city of Brownsville, Texas. Cartinas held the city captive for forty-eight hours and looted and murdered. The Rangers finally drove him back to Mexico, but not before he had committed many atrocities, including robbing and cattle stealing. Slade himself had nullified an abortive rising around Laredo.

There was no question but that the country south of the great river was misgoverned, with unwarranted privilege granted the wealthy and influential, the poor ground under the iron heel of a mistaken despot, who had himself started out as a *liberator* and for a while had accomplished much good — for a while.

Slade was convinced that eventually a true *liberator* would arise, a man of the people who would lay the foundation of the new, free, and strong Mexico that would stand shoulder to shoulder with America in the hour of trouble. But not yet.

Let such a man as Red Mike Talco come into power and the Border country of Texas would be drenched in blood, which Walt Slade earnestly hoped to prevent.

Of course there was a chance that he was merely a ruthless Border bandit, as most people appeared to consider him, a pest concurrent in the section. But there was also the chance that he might be considerably more than that. Slade had been impressed by the reckless courage of his followers; Talco seemed to have a genius for attracting the worst and most daring. The attempted drygulching of the sheriff's posse had evinced originality and careful planning.

Before long, Slade was to have another example of Red Mike's subtle ingenuity.

Knowing that he couldn't expect to be present every night, Slade had arranged for the faro dealer's assistant, who was also a capable dealer, to spell Crane Hodges at the big game when it was time for him to eat. Leaving the kitchen, after expressing his appreciation of the cook's cooperation, Slade spotted Hodges putting away a surrounding at a small corner table. He dropped into a chair opposite the dealer.

"Crane," he said, "I think it would be a good idea for you to keep a close watch on everything and to thoroughly familiarize yourself with the details of the business; may come in handy a little later."

Hodges' eyes widened. "You mean you may be willing to sell out, after a while?" he asked eagerly. Slade smilingly shook his head.

"Crane, I have nothing to sell," he replied. "I associated myself with the Golconda in deference to the request of a dying man."

"But Marshal willed his share of the place to you," Hodges protested.

"Yes, But I consider I hold it only in trust," Slade answered. "In trust for a good man who will be a help to Pete and stick with him at all times. You can interpret what I say as you please, but I think it would be a good idea for you to become conversant with all the details of the business. Incidentally, Pete and I discussed the matter, and we see eye to eye."

With a smile and a nod, he rose and sauntered to the end of the bar, where Black Pete stood. Hodges gazed after him, his face shining. His lips formed the inaudible words

"The whitest man that ever lived!"

Slade was on the dance floor, finishing a number with Mary, when two men bearing on their shoulders boxes marked, "Whiskey" entered. They had the appearance of truckers, but although the night was warm, both wore coats.

"Here you are, Pete," one called. "Looks like you're going to need it. We got more."

Pete opened the door to the back room and the men deposited their burdens on a table. One handed Pete a sheet of paper.

"We'll want you to check it against this list," he said. "Okay, we'll fetch the rest of it."

They hurried out, returned bearing more boxes, which they carried into the back room, one shutting the door behind them.

Their dance finished, Mary and Slade had returned to their table.

Several minutes passed and the two men did not reappear. Abruptly Slade stood up and crossed the room with long strides. At the back room door he hesitated a moment, then swung the door open to reveal a most unexpected tableau.

Black Pete stood rigid, his hands in the air. And with good reason; one of the "truckers" was holding a gun on him. His companion squatted beside the open safe, transferring its contents into a canvas sack.

The gunman whipped around at Slade's entrance, and fired point blank. But the instant before he squeezed the trigger, *El Halcon* drew and shot. The fellow crumpled up like a sack of old clothes. His companion surged erect, dodged behind Pete and, using him as a shield, fired over his shoulder.

The slug barely grazed Slade's jaw, but the shock hurled him momentarily off balance. The outlaw lined sights.

But Black Pete whirled. His great hands wrapped around the fellow's neck, the gun exploding harmlessly into the ceiling. Black Pete swept him off his feet and hurled him through the air. His head struck the edge of the safe door with a sodden crunch and he slid to the floor beside his dead companion. His limbs twitched a moment and were still.

"Thanks, Pete," Slade said, rubbing his tingling jaw. "That one was close."

Outside the door, pandemonium was utter and complete, men shouting and cursing, dance-floor girls shrieking, chairs overturning. The crowd surged toward the back room, Sheriff Traynor shouldering his way to the front, Mary Merril tagging along behind him, gun in hand.

"Take it easy," Slade advised, rolling a cigarette. "Everything is under control."

"What the blankety-blank happened?" howled the sheriff.

"Oh, the two gents just held up Pete and were cleaning the safe," Slade replied lightly. "Don't think they are in condition to try it again. Did you aim the hellion at the safe door, Pete? Cracked his skull like an egg shell."

The sheriff let out another indignant and injured howl.

"Dadblast you, I don't believe you've got a nerve in your body!" he stormed at Slade. "Pete, tell us what *did* happen?"

"Guess Mr. Slade just about told you," Black Pete replied. "As I started checking the list, one of them pulled a gun from under his coat and told me to elevate. I didn't argue."

"A darn good thing you didn't," growled the sheriff. "What next?"

"The other one hunkered down in front of the safe and laid his ear against the door and started twirling the knob," Pete replied.

90

"In less than a minute he had the door open. Then Mr. Slade came in and that was all."

"Yes, especially after Pete knocked the door hinges loose with that one over there," Slade added. "Looked like he'd grown wings; but he stopped flying mighty sudden."

"I don't know which is worse," grumbled the sheriff. "Don't 'pear a bit affected by what might easily have done for both of 'em."

"It didn't, and that's all that counts," Slade said lightly. "Right, Mary?"

"Let you out of my sight a minute and you're in trouble," she scolded, glaring at him as accusingly as if he had personally staged the affair for his own pastime. "You're the limit!"

The sheriff snorted agreement. "Okay, some of you guzzlers, pack the carcasses to my office so we can look 'em over in peace," he said. "Anybody remember seeing the horned toads before?"

Nobody did.

"All right, then, get going," Traynor ordered. "Don't want 'em left here cluttering up Pete's place."

"And now what?" he asked of Slade.

"Now we'll take a little look in the alley in

91

back," the Ranger said. "I'm pretty sure we'll find a couple of horses tethered there, all set for the get away after the safe was cleaned."

"And I had my brains pistol whipped out," said Pete, casting a grateful glance at Slade. "I figure that was just what would have happened."

Slade thought so, too, although he refrained from saying so. It was a vicious bunch.

As he opened the door that led to the alley, Slade glanced at the lock.

"Tomorrow we'll put up a couple of brackets and drop a bar across the door," he told Pete. "That old lock would present no obstacle to such a bunch as we are up against.

"I've a notion, though," he added thoughtfully, "that tonight we may have gotten rid of Talco's cracksman, and I doubt if he has another such on tap. Next time he'll very likely have to handle such a chore himself."

"Think he can do it?" Traynor asked curiously.

"Yes, I believe he can," Slade replied. "I venture to say he is thoroughly conversant with such matters; otherwise he would hardly have enlisted such a man. It wouldn't have occurred to him. As I said before, we are getting a new type of criminal. Yes, I believe if there is another safe opening chore to do, Talco may personally handle it. I could be mistaken, but perhaps not."

As Slade predicted, they found two horses tethered in the alley. Good-looking critters.

"We'll put 'em up for sale, along with the others," Traynor said. "Will pay for planting the devils. They would have made a good haul, wouldn't they?"

"Three days' take," Slade replied. "Pete planned to send it to the Alpine bank tomorrow. Yes, they would have done quite well. As smooth a scheme as I've ever heard tell of. Almost foolproof."

"How'd you catch on?" Traynor asked.

"I didn't, exactly, just sort of played a hunch," Slade replied. "I thought that pair was spending an undue time in the back room, and recalled that the last one in closed the door. All of a sudden, I figured I'd better have a look. And if it hadn't been for Pete's quick thinking and acting, it might have been my last look; that slug touching my jaw sort of knocked me off balance at the moment."

"How's your jaw feel?" Traynor asked.

"Nothing to bother about," Slade answered. "I managed to wipe most of the blood off before Mary got a look at close range."

"I think you'd better wipe it all off," the sheriff observed dryly.

Slade's lips twitched, but he passed up the rather pointed comment. Traynor made a shrewd remark.

"Wonder if a get-even notion had something to do with that raid?" he said. "Talco might have figured that cleaning the safe and pistol whipping Pete to death would be hitting at you."

"It is possible," Slade conceded. "I understand he had trouble with Ralph Marshal a while back."

"That's right," Traynor answered. "In a card game over to Hastings. Ralph caught him cold deckin' and called him on it. Talco went for his iron, but Ralph was mighty fast with a sleeve derringer he packed and shot it outa Talco's hand, along with a hunk of Talco's finger. Talco swore he'd get even. That was before he blossomed out as a full-fledged bandit. Yep, Talco is always out to even scores."

"If so, it is a weakness that may prove his undoing," Slade observed. "A yen for revenge sometimes clouds a man's judgment."

"Guess that's right," Traynor agreed. "Well, reckon we might as well take these nags with us to the rack in front of the office; Chumley can put them up. Make anything from the brands?"

"They sort of remind me of certain Arizona burns, but they have evidently been slick-iron altered. Have to take the hide off to find the original brand. Of no importance, anyhow. Let's go."

"And then back to the rumhole before your gal develops a case of the jitters," Traynor said.

When they reached the office, there were still some idlers hanging around discussing the happenings. Traynor shooed them out. Chumley, who had accompanied the bodies, looked after the horses.

"About on a par with the others we collected," was Slade's verdict after a close look at the dead faces. "It's a tough and salty bunch, all right, and somewhat smarter than the average, I'd say. Quite a bit smarter, in fact. Talco is undoubtedly blessed, or cursed, with imagination and knows how to put it to work. Looks like we've got *our* work cut out for us, Chet."

"Nothing new about that, so I ain't worrying," returned the sheriff. "Blazes! It's way past midnight! Your little gal must be dead on her feet. Just a minute and we'll go."

With which he went through the slain owlhoots' pockets, but unearthed nothing of importance save money, more than a little of it.

"Anyhow, the county treasury is getting rich," he commented as he pocketed the *dinero*.

Mary *was* tired when they reached the Golconda.

"I'm going upstairs," she announced. "Everybody is still noisy and excited, and I've had about all I can take for one day. I was in the saddle at dawn. Be seeing you both."

Black Pete gallantly held the door open for her, and made sure she had reached the stairhead before closing it.

"A fine lady," he said when he joined Slade and the sheriff. "Real Buckrah."

Which, Slade knew, was as fine a compliment as a Virginia-born Negro could pay.

"And very shortly I'm going in for a session of ear pounding," said Traynor. "First, though, a snort and a sandwich. Excitement always makes me hungry and thirsty. How about you, Walt?"

"I'll settle for another cup of coffee," the Ranger replied. "I think that will hold me."

"No sense in you staying up any longer than you feel like, Mr. Slade," said Pete. "I'll take care of everything and close up.

Crowd's beginning to thin out, anyhow; most of the boys have to work tomorrow."

"I'll see," Slade said, rolling another cigarette. Pete ambled off to check stock and attend to other chores. He turned back for a moment.

"Wonder how those robbers knew I was expecting a whiskey shipment tonight or in the morning?" he remarked.

"They seem to be able to learn anything they desire to," Slade replied. "Undoubtedly, Talco has men planted here in town, keeping a watch on things and on the lookout for possible prospects. He's clever, and far sighted, and has gotten together a bunch of better than average intelligence and that don't appear to have any conception of fear."

"Blasted wind spider," growled the sheriff, and lumbered upstairs to bed. Pete got busy with his chores.

Reversing his former mental decision, Slade sat on at the table, sipping coffee and smoking, and doing some hard thinking.

There was one refreshing angle, at variance with cases in which he had recently been involved; he knew exactly on whom to concentrate and was not forced to glean his quarry, a shadowy individual clothed with apparent respectability, from among a number of possible suspects. Red Mike undoubtedly headed his bunch, was the brains, the planner, the moving force. His chore was to eliminate Red Mike Talco.

Not that he underestimated that slippery individual. Talco had proven his ability and was quite likely a formidable opponent for even *El Halcon.* The puzzler, just exactly what was Talco up to? Did he plan to foment a Border uprising, under cover of which he would be able to nicely feather his own nest? Cheno Cartinas, and others, had done just that. The result, rapine and slaughter, the Border in a constant turmoil, innocent and misguided people killed. Slade earnestly hoped to prevent that.

He wondered just what was Talco's background, if Talco was his real name. Very likely it wasn't. Sheriff Traynor had intimated that he was a man of education and culture, perhaps the black sheep of a good family. And that type, it had been Slade's experience, was the very worst of the outlaw brand, often harboring bitter resentment for a wrong, real or fancied, an avowed enemy to all of decent humanity. Curly Bill Brocius, John Ringo, Doc Holliday, Billy the Kid, Jesse James, John Wesley Hardin — their name was legion.

Well, he'd been up against that sort before,

and had always managed to make out. Being honest with himself, he was forced to admit that he looked forward with a certain pleasurable anticipation toward the contest of brains and bullets with such a man.

Now the saloon was almost deserted. The bartenders sounded their last call. The faro bank was closed, the chips leveled off, as was the custom. The dealers were stowing away their cards. The floor girls and the musicians had departed. Ten minutes more and Pete shooed out the last stragglers and locked the door.

"I'm all ready to go, if you are, Mr. Slade," he said. "I sleep at the far end of the hall, last room on the left, if you should want me for anything."

"I'd like to have a look at your room," Slade replied.

Black Pete accompanied him to the neat and spotless chamber. Slade walked to the window and glanced out. The wall of the building was sheer, it was a good twenty feet to the ground, and there were no trees nearby.

"Not bad," he said, "but draw the shade, lock your door, and wedge a chair under the knob."

Pete looked startled. "You mean —" he hesitated.

"I mean only that we are up against a hard and vicious bunch and it's best not to take chances."

"How about you?" Pete asked apprehensively. Slade smiled.

"Nobody can touch a door without awakening me," he replied. "You see, Pete, I've had some experience with this sort of thing, and am always prepared."

"Guess that's right," Pete agreed. "Ain't anybody going to put something over on you."

"Hope not," Slade answered cheerfully. "Good night." He strolled down the hall, glancing to the left.

9

Sunshine and peace! That was Gato the following day. The sky was deepest blue. The mountain crests glittered in the golden light. Folks went about their business briskly. Even the eternal grumble and thud of the stamp mills seemed to have acquired a sprightly tone. Sunshine and peace! But far to the south was a black and lowering cloud that hovered just above the curve of the horizon.

Mary Merril, Slade, and Traynor had breakfast together around noon. She blushed rosily under the old sheriff's amused gaze.

"My, you look fresh as a daisy," he commented. "Smug as a cat outside a saucer of cream and with the canary's cage door open."

"Why not?" she retorted. "I had a good night's sleep."

"Hmmm!" said the sheriff.

Mary wrinkled her pert nose at him and requested more coffee.

"How would you like to look the stamp mill over?" Slade asked. "I want a word with Gord."

"I'd love to," she replied. "I've never been inside one. Sounds interesting."

After a final cup of coffee and a cigarette, Slade announced he was ready to go. They left the Golconda arm in arm, the sheriff's pleased smile following them.

Pete joined him for a moment. "A fine lady, a mighty fine lady," he said apropos of Mary Merril.

"Uh-huh, she is, well heeled, too," replied Traynor. "She owns half her uncle's big spread, the Cross W, up to the north of Sanderson, and a quarter interest in the carting business he and Pancho Arista operate. I think she and our young hellion would pull well in double harness, if he'd ever stop

101

gallivantin' all over the state long enough to get hitched."

Meanwhile, Slade and Mary had reached the mill, where Dick Gord, the manager, at once took the girl in tow, conducting her through the mill and explaining its workings.

The Contention mill was a six-stamp affair powered by steam. Six tall, upright rods of iron, larger than a man's arm, and heavily shod with iron and steel at their lower ends, were framed together like a gate. They rose and fell, one after the other, in a ponderous dance, in an iron box called a "battery." Each of the rods weighed more than seven hundred pounds. The masses of silver ore were broken up and shoveled into the battery. The dance of the stamps pulverized the rock to powder. A stream of water trickling into the battery turned it to a creamy paste. The smallest particles were driven through a fine wire screen that fitted close around the battery and washed into great tubs heated by steam. These tubs were called amalgamating pans.

The mass of pulp in the pans was kept constantly stirred up by revolving lumps of iron called mullers. Quicksilver was always kept in the battery. It seized some of the liberated gold and silver particles and held onto them. Quicksilver was also shaken into the pans at frequent intervals.

Streams of water flowed from the pans and were carried off in broad wooden troughs. Particles of gold and silver floated on the surface of the water and were caught by coarse blankets laid in the troughs, and little obstructions charged with quicksilver. Later the blankets and the riffles were washed of their precious accumulations. Once a week or so the stamps were stopped, the pulp in the pans and batteries freed of mud and dirt, leaving the mass of quicksilver with its imprisoned treasures. The mass of quicksilver was heated in a retort, the quicksilver passing off in form of vapor and leaving the gold and silver behind, usually a lump several times the size of a man's head. In the case of the Contention ore, more than a fifth of the mass was gold, although the color did not show, and would not have shown had two-thirds of it been gold.

All this Gord explained in an interesting manner to his pretty companion.

Slade, to whom a stamp mill was nothing new, wandered about the building. He found it boasted a large back door that was locked, barred, and bolted. Nothing short of a battering ram would open it from the outside. The windows were high, narrow, and barred with iron.

He made his way to the front entrance. The cook shanty was directly opposite, less than a half-score yards distant, the table so arranged that men eating had a clear view of the entrance. Nobody could pass through without being spotted. He shook his head and turned away. So far as he could see, the darn joint was impervious to a burglary attempt.

But nevertheless, he was playing a strong hunch that Mike Talco *did* contemplate a try for the payroll money, a large sum, which would be stashed away in the office safe. But how the devil would he work it?

Entering the office, he sat down in Gord's desk chair, rolled a cigarette, and pondered the problem, which appeared to defy solution, gazing absently at the big old iron safe in a far corner and out of line with the doors and windows.

Abruptly he realized that the desk in front of him was flooded with almost vertical rays of sunlight. He glanced up, and his lips pursed in a soundless whistle.

Directly over the desk was a wide skylight, now open, through which the sunlight was pouring. He stared at it, his brows drawing together.

By gosh, it could be done! Drop a rope

104

from the skylight. Active men could slide down it, clean the safe, and escape by way of the back door. No trouble to open that from the inside. Nor did gaining the roof of the building pose any great difficulty. Yes, it could be done!

He wondered if Mike Talco realized the possibility. Slade believed he did.

Rolling another cigarette, he began formulating a plan that might well rid the section of the pest, once and for all. That is if Talco decided to supervise the project in person, which he thought likely.

He felt pretty sure that Talco's wound had been but superficial and would doubtless be fairly well healed by now; not much of a handicap for a man of his rugged physique. Yes, there was a good chance Talco would take part in the chore.

Well, he had a couple of days to make ready a reception committee for *amigo* Talco, one the gentleman might not enjoy. He pinched out his cigarette and sauntered into the mill to look for Mary and Gord.

He found them watching the ceaseless dance of the stamps. The girl's eyes were bright with interest.

"It's fascinating," she said. "The darn things almost look alive."

"Like a hen on hot plates," he smiled.

"Not that I ever saw a hen on hot plates."

"If you did, you'd lift her off," Mary predicted. "Huh! There are times when I can sympathize with the hen."

"Lucky for you the sheriff isn't here," Slade said. "He would probably have made something of that remark."

"He's impossible, worse than you," Mary retorted. "Mr. Gord, won't you come over to the Golconda and have a drink with us?"

"Don't mind if I do," Gord accepted. "Guess they can do without me here for a short while."

"You two go ahead," Slade said. "I think Traynor is at his office now, and I wish a word with him."

"You're not gallivanting off somewhere?" Mary asked suspiciously.

"Nope," he replied. "I'll be seeing you soon."

Slade found the sheriff in his office, smoking his pipe and contemplating the two bodies on the floor.

"A couple of barkeeps think maybe they served them at one time or another," he replied to Slade's question as to possible recognition of the slain outlaws. "That's all. If anybody knows anything about them, they're keeping it to themselves. I've arranged to have them planted here. No sense in packing them to the county seat, where the coroner will want to hold an inquest, just a waste of time."

Slade nodded. Cow country, especially in the Big Bend, was lax where such things were concerned; didn't matter, anyhow.

Leaving Chumley, the deputy, to take care of any chance visitors, Slade and the sheriff repaired to the Golconda to join Mary and Gord, finding them comfortably ensconced at a table, Gord with a snort before him, Mary with a glass of wine Black Pete had recommended.

"The bouquet is wonderful," she said. "Pete is a connoisseur."

"Made from the golden grapes of the middle Rio Grande Valley, up toward El Paso," Slade said. "Without equal."

After a cup of coffee and a cigarette, Slade paid a visit to the kitchen for another talk with the old cook.

"*Capitan,*" Pedro said, "my *amigos* watch. Do men ride from the south, they will know, and report to me. Fear not, *Capitan,* their eyes are sharp and they know how to see and not be seen. The *amigos* of Juan, the orchestra leader, also has friends who watched, Yaqui-Mexicans, as is Juan, and *Capitan* know what that means."

"Yes," Slade agreed. "Knife men who can

split the spot on an ace of spade at twenty paces with a blade. Does Talco meddle with them we won't have to bother about Talco any more."

"*Si*, it is so," said Pedro.

Confident that Red Mike and his bunch would be unable to enter Gato without the fact being known and relayed to him, Slade returned to his table and sat down with more coffee. Mary regarded him suspiciously.

"You're looking mighty smug," she said. "I've a notion you are up to something."

"Not at present, anyhow," he returned lightly.

Gord asked Mary to dance, and while they were on the floor, Slade acquainted the sheriff with what he discovered in the mill.

"And you really think they might try it that way?" Traynor asked dubiously.

"It's that way or not at all," Slade replied. "There is absolutely no other way to enter that office unobserved. I'm playing a hunch that if I noted the possibility, Talco did, too."

"You and your hunches!" grumbled the sheriff. "But the darn things always seem to work out."

"I know it sounds ridiculous," Slade admitted, "but I feel it is the sort of thing that would appeal to his crafty and devious mind. On a par with the try for the Golconda money."

"And what are we going to do about it?"

"Right now I don't know," the Ranger admitted frankly. "There is no place to hole up in the office, nor in the mill so far as I was able to see. We would have to cross a wide, open space where we would be sure to be spotted by anyone keeping a watch in the office. And you can rest assured that Talco would be keeping watch. We'd be settin' quail. Well, I'll have to browse about a little more and see if I can unearth something. When Gord leaves, I'll walk with him. You keep Mary here. I want to have a look at the grounds surrounding the mill. Perhaps I can spot something I overlooked."

"You'll figure a way," Traynor declared confidently. "No doubt in my mind as to that."

"Here's hoping you're playing it straight," Slade smiled. "Right now, as the old saying goes, 'I'm up a stump.' Well, we'll see."

"And you figure Talco himself will be on the job?"

"Yes, I do," *El Halcon* replied. "That's why I'm so anxious to make a go of it. May provide opportunity to make a clean sweep of the whole blasted bunch before they murder somebody else; they're killers. And if Pedro, the cook, is correct in his surmise, it may prevent an abortive Border rising that could mean trouble a-plenty. We can well do without that."

"You're darn right," agreed Traynor. "That's always something that must be considered in this blankety-blank section."

Mary and Gord finished their dance and returned to the table, where the manager had a last drink.

"Have to be getting back on the job," he said. "We're making ready for the weekly clean-up and I always like to supervise that. See you later in the evening, I hope."

"I'll walk with you," Slade said. Mary shook her head resignedly, but offered no objections.

In the course of the walk to the mill, Slade briefly recounted what he believed to be in the wind. Gord looked decidedly startled.

"Do you think I should put somebody in the office to keep a watch on things," he asked. "The money will be there day after tomorrow."

Slade instantly vetoed this suggestion.

"In the first place, it would be taking a chance on getting him killed," he pointed out. "They must have somebody else planted in the mill to take care of just such a contingency. Besides, I'm anxious to catch the devils red-handed. They won't get the money, I promise you that."

"Then I reckon I have nothing to worry about," Gord said in relieved tones. "Okay, handle it as you see fit; I'll cooperate in any way you suggest. Now what?"

"Now I'm going to give the grounds around the mill a once-over and try and figure some way to get the jump on the hellions."

After Gord had entered the mill, Slade sauntered about. Among other things, he came upon a shed where several long ladders were stored. By means of one, the roof of the mill could easily be reached. Something else Red Mike quite likely knew about.

He surveyed the roof of the building. It was a good thirty feet from the ground. The skylight, he noted, rested on a cupola or dome some five or six feet in height above the roof proper. He studied it thoughtfully, deciding that it offered possibilities.

"Yes, it might work," he mused aloud. "About the only thing I see that could. Well, I've a notion it's worth a try."

His plan had now assumed more definite shape; it was still somewhat faulty, something in the nature of a gamble, with lives at stake, but he resolved to give it a whirl. He returned to the Golconda, where Mary and the sheriff awaited him.

10

The following day, a Sunday, passed without incident. Early Monday afternoon, Dick Gord contacted Slade.

"Well, the money's in the safe, awaiting a greedy hand," was his jocular remark.

"I think you can depend on it staying there safe until the boys get their paws on it, after which I refuse to predict its ultimate fate," Slade replied.

"I can tell you," was the pessimistic rejoinder. "The saloonkeepers, the card sharps, and the floor girls will get rich."

"Could be," Slade agreed cheerfully. "They have to live, too."

Gord grunted, and did not appear favorably impressed.

A little later, Pedro, the cook, poked his nose out the kitchen and nodded to Slade. The Ranger joined him.

"Capitan," Pedro said, "men ride from the south, five in number. Talco? That my *amigos* did not know; they feared to get too close."

"Good judgment," Slade said. *"Gracias,* Pedro, you're a big help." He immediately informed the sheriff.

"I think you, Chumley, and myself should be able to handle the situation," he said. "If things work out as I plan, we should have the big advantage of surprise in our favor. I don't think even *amigo* Talco, shrewd as he is, will guess what we have in mind. If he does make a try, I feel we will get the jump on him without difficulty."

"Certain," agreed Traynor. "I figure the horned toad is in for the surprise of his ornery life, and maybe the last one."

Shortly before dark, Slade, the sheriff, and the deputy rode out of town and turned east, destination unknown, so far as Gato was concerned. Slade made sure they were not followed, then circled around to approach the mill from the west.

"If the devils happen to have been keeping tab on us in town, which is possible, this should throw them off," Slade said.

Finally, they sighted the mill, looming gaunt against the star-strewn sky. In a convenient grove nearby, they tethered their horses and with the greatest caution, pausing often to peer and listen, they approached the building. Slade bore with him his sixty-foot manila twist rope.

Without making the slightest noise, they slid one of the ladders from the shed and by means of it reached the mill roof. Slade looped the rope around the top rung, pushed the ladder away from the wall, and gently lowered it to the ground, drawing the rope back.

"I'd say they are almost sure to ascend by way of the back wall," he breathed to his companions. "Even did they stumble over the darn thing, they'd surely have to be omniscient to guess why it happened to be there."

Silently, they stole across to the skylight cupola. Slade secured the rope to one of the bars and coiled it beside the dome, through which light poured up from the office below. Against the sides of the dome, however, was black shadow. Knowing he would be invisible from below and confident his amazingly keen hearing would instantly detect any attempt to mount to the roof, he took up his post where he could see the open door of the cook shanty.

A long and tedious wait followed. The monotonous drumming of the stamps had a soporific effect and Slade could hardly keep his eyes open. The sheriff and Chumley did snooze comfortably seated on the roof, their backs against the cupola wall.

Finally the stamps abruptly ceased their grumbling, and the silence that followed was deafening, broken only by the voices of the men streaming from the mill to the cook shanty.

"Get set," Slade whispered to his companions. "If it's going to happen, it will be any minute now."

After a tense interval, with every sense at hairtrigger alertness, Slade's ears caught a slight scraping sound coming from the back of the building. Another moment and the form of a man loomed shadowy against the stars. Another followed, another, another, and still another, drifting silently toward the skylight. Slade nudged Traynor. The sheriff's voice rang out:

"Elevate! You're covered!"

There was a storm of startled exclamations. Slade sensed rather than saw the grab for weapons. He drew and shot with both hands.

A gasping cry echoed the reports, followed by a choking grunt and a queer thrashing about on the shingles.

Traynor and Chumley were also shooting as fast as they could squeeze trigger. Answering gushes of flame sent slugs thudding into the cupola, zinging from the skylight bars. Slade felt the wind of passing bullets, felt the burn of one along the side of his neck. He fired again and again. Another cry sounded, a curse from the sheriff. Slade saw a huge form loom against the stars at the rear of the mill roof. Then it vanished from sight. Another flickered after it. He raced forward, guns ready for instant action, stumbled over a body, caught his balance after a moment of floundering.

In back of the mill sounded a muffled thump, another. Then the rattling and scraping of a ladder sliding along the mill wall. With a muttered oath, he raced back to the skylight, flung the coiled rope through the wide opening and slid down it so fast it smoked. He thudded onto the desk top, reeled, caught his balance once again, leaped to the floor, and scudded out the mill door. Swerving around the corner of the building at a dead run, he slewed sideways as a gun blazed, the slug coming close. He fired at the flash, heard a bubbling shriek and lined sights with a dimly seen man swinging onto the back of a horse. But both triggers clicked on empty shells. The horseman vanished in the darkness to the accompaniment of drumming hoofs. Thoroughly disgusted, *El Halcon* reloaded with speed. However, there was nothing more to shoot at.

The cook shanty was a bedlam of yells and curses and questions. Slade's great voice cut through the turmoil.

"Fetch lanterns," he shouted. "Get a move on!"

That thundering voice got order, or something resembling it. Another moment and lights flickered, coming toward him, cautiously.

From the roof top sounded more profanity.

"We got three up here!" Sheriff Traynor bawled. "You all right, Walt?"

"Fine as frog hair," the Ranger called back. "I think I have one down here."

Taking a proferred lantern, he moved ahead, gun ready for business. It wasn't needed. There was a dead man on the ground, blood still flowing from his bullet-slashed throat. It was not Red Mike Talco.

"How the blankety-blank we going to get down from here?" bellowed the sheriff. "I don't aim to slide down that blankety-blank rope like you did; liable to bust a leg. And Chumley packs so much tallow, if he happened to fall he'd starve before he stopped bouncing."

"Have a ladder up to you in a minute," Slade called in reply. He led the chattering crowd back to the rear wall of the mill. Lying beside it was a ladder, all right, and, glancing at it, Slade was confident that neither of the three dead men on the roof was Red Mike Talco. With his brain working at lightning speed, Talco had taken time to throw down the ladder, hoping thus to foil pursuit — which was just what he did.

"A bunch trying to lift your payroll money," Slade replied to the questions of the excited mill workers. "They didn't get it." There was a moment of silence, then a loud cheer as the welcome information soaked in. A lantern was held close.

"It's Mr. Slade!" a voice shouted. "Hurrah for Mr. Slade!" A still louder cheer sounded.

"Place the ladder against the wall," Slade told his well wishers. "I'm coming up," he called to the sheriff and ascended to the roof bearing one of the lanterns, by the light of which the bodies scattered about were examined.

"Nope, none of 'em Talco," said Traynor, adding a few choice expletives directed at the not present Red Mike.

"Yes, he made it in the clear," Slade said. "I might have gotten him if my guns hadn't picked such an inopportune moment to go empty. He thinks like a streak of goose grease in a hurry, and the devil's own luck seems to ride with him. Say, didn't I hear you let out a beller, Chet? Did you catch one?"

"Nicked my arm, nothing to bother about," replied the sheriff.

"Let's have a look," Slade said. The sheriff drew up his sleeve.

The wound indeed proved trifling, not much more than a graze.

"Take care of it after a bit," Slade said. "Blazes! Looks like everybody in town is showing up. Not standing room down there. Well, guess we'd better descend and greet the populace. Something seems to have them a mite excited. We'll let the workers pack the bodies down."

When they reached the ground, Dick Gord was the first to meet them. He solemnly shook hands with Slade.

"You sure called your shots," he said. "Worked out just as you figured it would. But you'd better hustle over to the Golconda and — no, you don't need to, here she is now."

It was indeed Mary Merril, with Black Pete looming beside her like an ebony guardian angel.

"She would come when we heard the shooting," he explained to Slade. "Figured I'd better come along to look after her, just in case."

"Thanks, Pete," Slade replied. "A good

119

thing you did; she might have got stepped on."

"You!" she stormed at him, and turned to Gord. "Now do you see what I meant when I said I could sympathize with a hen on hot plates?" she asked. "I'm always on them!"

"I don't think you need bother your pretty head about him," Gord rejoined. "He can take care of himself." Mary did not appear completely reassured.

"Some of you fellows go up and pack the bodies down," Slade said to the mill workers. "And while you're at it, untie my rope from the skylight and drop it on the desk."

"We'll take care of it, Mr. Slade," answered several voices.

Another ladder was fetched and the workers swarmed to the roof.

"Hey, Mr. Slade, there's another rope up here, a nice long one," somebody shouted.

"Throw it down," Slade directed. The coil smacked on the ground.

"The one by which they intended to reach the office through the skylight," Slade remarked. "A good twine. Next locate their horses; figure they're tethered in the trees over to the east. More *dinero* for your county treasury. Chances are there is still more in the dead men's pockets." That proved to be the case.

"Pack 'em to my office," said the sheriff.

"And everybody take an extra hour off to finish eating," shouted Gord, to the accompaniment of another cheer.

Townspeople clustered around the bodies, peering, exclaiming, this time with better results than formerly. A number of citizens recalled seeing one or another of the outlaws hanging around town.

"Never seemed to bunch up, though," somebody remarked. "Sorta played it lone wolf style."

"That way they would attract little notice," Slade explained. "A shrewd bunch, all right. Wonder how many more there are left? Not that such a leader as Talco will have much trouble enlisting recruits. Plenty of that sort in the section."

"Thick as blackberries," growled a bar owner. "Well, at this rate there won't be so many left, thanks to Mr. Slade and our sheriff."

The horses ridden by the slain owlhoots were discovered tethered among the trees to the east, good-looking critters with, as usual, slick-ironed brands. They were headed to the stables.

A long ladder was procured, on which the bodies were laid end to end. Eager volunteers started a triumphal march to the sheriff's office.

"Guess we might as well round up our nags and stable them," Slade said. "Nothing more we can do here, so far as I can see."

"You did enough," Dick Gord declared heartily.

Retrieving his rope from the office, Slade put it where it belonged and mounted Shadow, swinging Mary Merril up before him.

"Cozy as the first time you met me," she said, snuggling close in his arms. "I like to ride this way. And now that all is over, I'm feeling a mite shakey. And I'm sure I've acquired a few more gray hairs."

"Sure don't show," Slade told her as a street light under which they passed glinted on her bright curls.

"Oh, I manage to keep them covered up, so far," Mary said. "But if you keep on the way you are going, that condition won't last for long."

He dropped her off at the Golconda, stabled Shadow, and accompanied the sheriff to his office, where the bodies were neatly laid out, with folks giving them a once-over. Shortly after, Dick Gord dropped in.

"I'm letting the boys knock off a couple of hours early to make ready for their payday bust," he said. "Just the same, I'm taking no chances. I've got four men with rifles posted around the grounds, out of sight. They'll stay there till the safe is empty."

"I don't think you have anything to worry about," Slade assured him. "I don't credit even Talco for having the nerve to stage a raid single-handed."

"I wouldn't put anything past him," Gord growled. "You feel sure he was the one that escaped, that it was really Talco?"

"I'm convinced it was. I got a look at his size and shape as he went over the edge of the roof. Of course, I couldn't go into a court of law and swear it was Talco. In fact, I really have nothing on Talco that would stand up in court."

"How about the murder of Ralph Marshal?"

"Talco was more than two hundred yards distant when he turned his horse," Slade replied. "Convincing a jury, always an uncertain quantity, that I recognized a man on a galloping horse, more than two hundred yards distant, would be a considerable chore. Very likely a good lawyer would get him off."

"Guess you're right," Gord admitted. He chuckled.

"You've sure got yourself in solid with my

boys," he explained. "Were it not for you, there would very likely have been no payday for them tomorrow, and they've been looking forward to it for a month."

Slade cared for the sheriff's wound, which really was trifling. After, they closed up shop for a while and went in search of something to eat.

Gato was wild with excitement over the frustration of the robbery attempt, and in the crowded Golconda, it was the chief topic under discussion. Slade was showered with praise and congratulations and the sheriff and Chumley were not neglected.

"Guess the hellions are learning there ain't any easy pickings in this pueblo, any more," an oldtimer summed up.

Slade was not so optimistic.

But excitement is wearying and by an hour or so after midnight, the crowd was pretty well thinned out. Ahead was the big day, with not only the mines but several of the nearer ranches paying off. Mary trotted off to bed. Pete sounded his last call.

"Folks are all hepped up over what happened," remarked the sheriff as he sampled his final snort. "Just the same, though, they're a mite jittery. The other stamp mill is swarming with guards, I was told. Hope they don't go loco and shoot each other.

Personally, I'm of the notion that *amigo* Talco has a bellyful for a while."

"He has suffered a couple of setbacks, that's all," Slade corrected. "I doubt if he is much affected. He knows he can't win them all and reacts accordingly. He'll cut loose somewhere, and soon, is my opinion. Our chief chore is to try and anticipate his next move. If we don't I fear it will be accompanied by a killing or two. I expect he is in a killing mood about now."

"With you as the prime target," said Traynor.

Slade shrugged his broad shoulders.

"Could be," he concurred carelessly. "If he grows too impetuous, he might slip. Well, I'm going to bed. Pete has given me the nod and is closing up."

"Me, too, as soon as I finish my snort," said the sheriff. "Be seeing you."

11

The Contention was the biggest mine in the section, and the best producer, but there were others, and all were doing well. The Monarch of the Mountains, as it was grandiloquently named, for instance, had its own small stamp mill. So when all the workers received their monthly wage and knocked off for a day and a night, Gato really howled.

All the Gato saloons did an excellent business but, since Slade's advent, the Golconda topped them all.

It was not only because he liked the excitement and hilarity that Slade frequented the saloon. In fact, there were times when he could do with a little less of both. But in a mining and cow town, there was no other place so productive of information. A face, a chance word, a gesture, each and every one might be fraught with significance, and alcohol loosens tongues.

Before noon, cowhands from the neighborhood spreads were racing their horses along the dusty streets, singing and whooping. A steady stream of workers filed into the offices, and emerged with money burning holes in their pockets. The bar owners, the floor girls, and the gamblers would do their best to prevent a conflagration, and usually succeeded.

Also, opportunity might be provided for gentlemen of easy conscience and share-the-wealth notions. Slade was sure that Red Mike Talco was one of their number and would quite likely take advantage of anything that promised profit.

So before going down to breakfast, Slade sat by the window smoking, and endeavoring to surmise what Red Mike might have in mind, if anything, and to, if possible, forestall it. He conned over various prospects that might appear attractive to the outlaw leader. The saloons would be bursting with money, but saloons were not easy to take over, especially on payday nights, when the owners were very much on the alert. The big general store would also be loaded, the more prudent of the workers making needed purchases before drinking. But there the same conditions prevailed, everybody on their toes and prepared against emergencies.

If Talco did make a try, it would be something clever, subtle, out of the ordinary. But Red Mike appeared to thrive on the difficult and the unexpected; that was his past history, so far as Slade had been able to learn, and it was unlikely that he had changed.

There was one thing Slade believed counted in his favor. Right now, Talco was doubtless in a black rage, and itching to even the score with the man who had three times outwitted him. Four times, in fact, counting his original brush with the outlaw. And his bitter anger might cloud his judgment and cause him to become unduly reckless.

After arriving at this fairly satisfactory

conclusion, Slade pinched out his cigarette and descended to breakfast.

He had given his order and was sipping a cup of coffee the waiter had thoughtfully provided to sustain him while the food was being prepared, when Mary flounced down and flopped into a chair, announcing she was starved.

"A normal condition, though," she added. "When I'm not, I'll have to stop worrying about my figure and concentrate on something else."

"Haven't heard any complaints, yet, have you?" he countered.

"No, not so far," she admitted, "but they say the eyes of love are blind. I hope they are, and are."

"That one is a trifle difficult to untangle," he said.

"It shouldn't be," she retorted. "Well, here goes for another pound or two."

Sheriff Traynor rolled in to join them, glancing around the already crowded room.

"Going to be a heller," he predicted, apropos of the coming night. "Never saw folks so hopped up and ready to raise the roof. Liable to be some business before morning. Oh, well, if it is just honest ruckuses, we can handle 'em without any trouble. I've swore in three specials, fellers I

128

can depend on. They'll take care of minor shenanigans and we can concentrate on what might prove serious."

"I know I'm going to love this night, that is if I can keep you and Walt from gallivanting off somewhere," Mary said.

"We'll try and sit tight," the sheriff reassured her. "But don't forget, trouble just nacherly follows him around. Try to keep your thumb on him and maybe he'll make out. Let us drink!"

After he finished eating, and had his final cup of coffee and a cigarette, Slade gave Pete a hand, for business was really picking up. As an afterthought, he pulled Crane Hodges out of the poker game and ordered his substitute to take over.

"You stay on the floor tonight," he told the big head dealer. "You might be needed."

"That's a notion, all right," Hodges agreed. "No telling what may cut loose once the redeye begins to really get the boys going. You can depend on me, Mr. Slade."

"I arrived at that conclusion some time ago, Crane," *El Halcon* replied smilingly.

"Now," he added, "I think I'll mosey out and look the town over a bit."

First, however, he returned to the table for a word with Mary and the sheriff.

"You watch your step," Traynor cautioned

when he informed them of what he had in mind.

"Don't think there's anything to worry about in broad daylight," he replied lightly.

"Don't be so sure," grunted the sheriff. "That devil is full of surprises."

The girl's eyes were anxious as they followed his tall form through the swinging doors.

Although it still lacked some hours until dark, Gato's streets were gay and animated. Everybody appeared to have cast off their cares, if they had any, and were evidently bent on having a good time. To heck with tomorrow! It may never come, for some of us. And who knows but what his number is up!

The sky was clear blue, for with the mills shut down and the fires under the boilers banked only an occasional wisp of smoke drifted from the tall chimneys. The dark cloud that usually lowered over the town was conspicuous by its absence.

But once again, Slade noted that black and ominous drift rising slowly back of the mountains and seeming to draw their threatening crags with it.

An omen of evil now on its way? He laughed at the droll conceit, and continued his stroll with a carefree mind.

130

He paused before the big general store, which was doing plenty of business, and studied the building carefully, noting that the windows were barred, the front door massive and double-locked. Didn't look like a good prospect for a gentleman like Red Mike Talco.

But recalling the ingenuity displayed in the try for the Contention payroll money, he was not positive; appearances might be deceptive.

The store fronted on a quiet side street that at night was deserted, or nearly so. It backed on a narrow alley. Slade turned the corner and sauntered down the alley, pausing beside the rear door of the store. It was solidly built, but a single glance at the keyhole told him the lock was an old-fashioned one that would pose little difficulty for such an expert as Mike Talco.

But he had learned from the sheriff that there would be a watchman inside the store at night with a sawed-off shotgun and other weapons ready to hand. A sturdy oldtimer, a former Sieber scout, who would not likely be taken unawares. And to reach the office and the safe, anybody entering from the rear would have to cross a fairly wide, open space. No, it still didn't look like a good prospect.

Nevertheless, the indefinable something he termed a hunch was stirring in his brain. He glanced about, noted that almost directly opposite the door was a narrow opening between two buildings, an excellent hole-up for anybody interested in the store. He walked back up the alley, deep in thought.

For some time, Slade wandered about town, entering various places, talking with the owners and others, and learning nothing. But the hunch persisted, even seemed to grow stronger, until he was convinced that before the night was over, something would be pulled at the general store. What? How? He didn't know; hadn't the slightest notion.

But, he mused morosely, little doubt but that Red Mike Talco knew exactly what *he* was going to do. That was where he had the advantage. He *knew,* while Slade could only try and guess.

The sun sank in sullen splendor, wreathed by vapors, and very quickly it was dark. The somber cloud bank to the south had now climbed to the zenith, blotting out the stars, and slowly, slowly crept over the bustling town, where infrequent street lights flickered and windows glowed golden, beckoning to the crowd that thronged the board sidewalks and grew more hilarious by the minute.

In an irritated mood Slade made his way to the Golconda, where he found Mary and the sheriff anxiously awaiting him.

"Pedro, the cook, wants to see you," Traynor said. "Seems to be worked up about something."

Without delay, Slade entered the kitchen. Pedro led him to a little table in a corner, poured him a cup of coffee, and sat down.

"*Capitan,*" he said, keeping his voice very low, "again men ride from the south, three in number this time. My *amigos* watched and saw."

He glanced around, lowered his voice still more.

"And, *Capitan,*" he added sententiously, "this time they are sure that one is the *ladrone,* Talco the accurst."

"*Gracias,* Pedro, and *gracias* to your *amigos;* that is what I hoped to hear. You are a real help."

"To serve *El Halcon,* the just, is the honor great," said Pedro.

When he returned from the kitchen, Traynor gave him a searching look, and so did Mary, but they asked no questions. They knew he would talk only when ready.

He did not mention what he was debating in his mind. For if he decided to play his hunch, he preferred to do it lone-wolf style.

And the hunch was steadily growing stronger. Just how he would work it, he still didn't know for sure, but a plan was taking form. A problematical and hazardous plan, but one he believed had a chance to work if *amigo* Talco would just "cooperate" a little. He knew the store would close around ten o'clock, so while he lent Pete a hand with his multitudinous duties he kept an eye on the clock.

Dick Gord appeared and joined them. He gazed around complacently at the animated scene.

"Looks like the boys are already feeling their oats a mite," he observed. "Well, they've got it coming to them; they work hard and don't shirk. I shoved a few extra pesos into each pay envelope — figured it was due them, everything considered, so they are well heeled."

"A nice thing to do," Slade said, "and I'm sure the boys appreciate it. Well, there's the head bartender waving for more stock. Be seeing you."

He took up his post at the end of the bar, near the till, while Pete selected needed bottles for a swamper to hustle out. Hodges was circulating through the crowd, as was another floor man. Everything appeared to be under control. Glancing at the clock, he saw it registered 9:30. Fifteen minutes more he'd make his move.

The minutes passed swiftly, 9:45 said the clock. Mary and Gord were dancing, the sheriff alone at his table. Slade paused beside him for a moment, waved to Mary.

"Don't leave," he told Traynor. "Might send for you."

Before the sheriff could protest, he was out the swinging doors.

With swift strides, Slade headed for the vicinity of the general store. He reached the dark alley and entered it; undoubtedly it was deserted. He glided down it to the narrow opening between the building just a little up the lane from the store's back door.

Although he did not expect to find anybody in the opening, he approached it warily, peering and listening. Reassured by the continued silence, and lack of movement, he slipped into the crack which, as he expected, proved to be unoccupied. Taking up his post at the outer edge of the opening, he fixed his gaze on the dimly seen mouth of the alley.

The slow minutes dragged past with nothing happening. Then abruptly three shadowy figures materialized in the mouth of the alley. *El Halcon* tensed for instant action.

However, the three men did not come up

the alley. Instead, they lounged in its mouth in an attitude of waiting. Slade's eyes never left them.

Meanwhile, an elderly, sedate-appearing gentleman was just turning the corner into the street, which ran past the alley mouth and on to the lighted business section. It was Clifton Standish, the manager of the Gato General Store, last to leave the building.

He walked slowly, reviewing the problems of the busy day. He reached the alley mouth and a man stepped out, directly behind him. He did not need to be told that the hard something jammed against his ribs was the muzzle of a gun.

"Hold it!" said the gunman, his voice soft, low. Standish halted.

"Back the way you came," said the gunman. "No tricks if you wish to stay alive."

Standish obeyed; there was nothing else for him to do, for in that soft voice was a deadly threat. As he moved up the street, the gunman beside him and a little to the rear, two more men emerged from the alley and sauntered along in his wake, dropping back a bit as they approached the corner.

"Straight to the front door of the store, identify yourself to the fellow in there, and tell him to open the door," his captor directed, the pale gleam from a distant street light glinting on his red hair.

Standish didn't argue the point; he knew he was caught settin', and if he disobeyed, his life wouldn't be worth a plugged peso — in that he was definitely right. He hammered on the door and called out, trying to keep his voice steady:

"It's me, Milt — Mr. Standish. Open up, I forgot something."

There was a rasp of keys in locks, the door swung open, and the watchman looked squarely into the muzzle of a second gun Red Mike Talco had instantly produced.

"Up!" Talco ordered. "Face the wall with your hands against it. Stay that way if you want to stay alive."

The watchman obeyed, for he, too, was caught settin'. Seething inwardly he faced the wall as two more men entered, guns ready for business.

"Close the door," Talco said. "No, don't lock it; we might need it in a hurry.

"You," he told Standish, "open that safe and be quick about it. Here, I'll push that table and the lamp closer. Get busy!"

Standish was white and trembling, but the former Sieber scout's face was fiery red, his eyes glaring. Fear was not the emotion that swayed *him,* but bitter humiliation at being caught in such a trap. With shaking hands, Standish got busy on the safe.

12

Walt Slade had been too far away to hear what was said, or to see just what was done in the gloomy alley mouth. To all appearances, the three men had been awaiting a fourth, who had arrived. But why did they turn down the street instead of up the alley toward the back door of the store? He didn't know, but resolved to try and find out. Whisking down the alley, he slowed at its mouth, listened a moment, then eased ahead until he could see around the corner of the building; the street was deserted. He hesitated another instant, then moved swiftly down the street, pausing still again at the corner. Peering around the edge of the building, he saw that the street that ran past the store entrance was also deserted. It was a rather long street and he did not think the four men had had time to reach the far corner unless they speeded up sharply. He glided along the front of the store.

A rather dim light glowed back of the window. The front door was closed. Slade paused directly outside it. To his keen ears came a mutter of voices. Again he hesitated, then reached out, seized the knob, and gently turned it. He felt the bolt slide back; the door was not locked.

For an instant he paused. Were just legitimate business going on behind that door, he would look like an utter fool; but he had a feeling that whatever was going on was *not* legitimate. He flung the door wide open, whipped inside, and instantly understood.

As he entered, with a startled shout, a man whirled toward him, gun jutting forward. Slade drew and shot with both hands. The fellow rocked back on his heels and thudded to the floor. Slade, weaving, slithering, ducking, swung his guns around to line sights with Red Mike Talco. But before he could bring them to bear, Talco's great arm shot out and swept the lamp from the table. Darkness blanketed the room, gushes of flame blasting through it. Slade felt the wind of passing bullets; one fairly whispered in his ear. He fired again and again.

Standish was yelling in terror, the watchman raving curses. Through the uproar, Slade heard a patter of steps toward the rear of the store. He fired in the direction of the sound, leaped forward, and collided with the cursing watchman. Before he could untangle himself, he heard a key click in a lock, a door bang shut. He rushed toward the back entrance, heedless of possible obstacles, groped a moment, and seized the door knob.

It resisted his efforts. He hit the door once with his shoulder, but the stout barrier didn't even creak.

"Get a light going!" he roared to the pandemonium up front.

The yelling and cursing stilled. A match scratched, its tiny flicker was touched to the wick of a bracket lamp; a mellow glow flooded the office and the front of the store. Slade holstered his guns and started rolling a cigarette.

"Got away," answered the questions hurled at him. "The nerve of that sidewinder! Took time to lock the door from the outside; he never misses a bet."

"Who — who was it?" quavered the store manager.

"Red Mike Talco and a couple of his horned toads," Slade replied laconically.

The manager stared and blinked. "You're Mr. Slade, Sheriff Traynor's new deputy, aren't you?" he asked. Slade nodded.

"And I think, Mr. Slade, that we both owe it to you for being alive," Standish said slowly, his voice still not steady. "The chances are he would have killed us before leaving."

Slade thought it probable.

"Well, anyhow he's short one of his bunch," he remarked, glancing at the body on the floor. He turned to the watchman who was still mumbling cuss words, largely directed at himself.

"Hustle up to the Golconda and tell Sheriff Traynor I said to come down here," he ordered. "And tell him and the lady with him that I'm okay."

"Certainly," said the watchman, and darted out on an errand. Standish glanced after him.

"You don't think there's a chance those devils might come back?" he asked apprehensively.

"I wish they would, but they won't," Slade replied grimly. "No, Talco knows when he's packed a licking; you won't see any more of him tonight. Now suppose you tell me just what happened." The manager related the details of his capture. Slade nodded thoughtfully.

"They evidently had been keeping tabs on your movements, which I imagine are fairly routine," he said. "Knew you would be the last to leave the store, and what time. A shrewd devil and farsighted. Luck sort of broke against him tonight."

"I have another name for it," Standish replied.

Slade sat down and rolled another cigarette. "See they didn't have time to tie onto the money," he commented, glancing at the closed safe. "No, thanks to you," Standish replied. "A tidy sum in there, too. I feel that you are due an adequate reward. I'll —"

El Halcon smilingly shook his head. "Thank you, sir," he interrupted, "but the opportunity to put one over on the devil is reward enough."

Standish regarded him a moment, and did not press his point.

Outside, hurried steps sounded. Standish started in his chair, but Slade kept on puffing his cigarette.

Sheriff Traynor burst in, Dick Gord and Mary Merril following him.

"Hello, Standish," Gord greeted the store manager. "Gather you've been having a mite of excitement down here."

"More than I ever want to have again," Standish replied, with feeling. "I'm not cut out for such goings-on."

"To tell the truth, I'm not either," Gord admitted. "But Walt here seems to thrive on it. Everything under control, eh, Walt?"

"And you got another one of the hellions," said Traynor. "This ain't so bad."

"But Talco made it in the clear, per usual," Slade replied.

"Well, let's have it," Traynor urged. "The watchman told us some, but not all. Incidentally, Standish, I told him to have a couple of snorts before he came back to work; I'm of the notion he needed 'em."

"He's not the only one" Standish said heartily. "I figure we'll all have a few together, a little later."

He was introduced to Mary who regarded him speculatively, doubtless sensing possible carting business.

"Let's have it, Walt," Traynor repeated. "Suppose just a case of all the luck coming your way, to hear you tell it."

"Not altogether," Slade said, with a wry smile. "As I told you, Talco escaped."

The sheriff put out his favorite remark, "just a matter of time. Okay, go ahead."

Briefly, Slade recounted the incidents. Standish expanded the happenings in the office, not at all to Slade's discredit. The sheriff chuckled; Mary sighed resignedly.

"I'll have that carcass packed to my office, Cliff, no sense in it cluttering up the premises," Traynor assured the store manager. "First let me take a glim at the hellion's pockets. Ha! Plenty of *dinero;* business is good."

Slade spared hardly a glance at what the pockets uncovered, knowing that Mike Talco would not permit his men to pack anything that might prove of value to a law-enforcement officer.

The night watchman appeared shortly, his temper apparently somewhat improved by his libations, and took over, his shotgun ready for any eventuality.

"It ain't getting outa my hand all night," he declared. "Just let somebody else try to bust in here!"

"Don't shoot my boys when they come for the carcass," Traynor admonished him. "I'll tell 'em to beller loud before they touch the door. All set? Let's go!"

"Yes, as you said, the devil's own luck seems to ride with that hellion," he observed to Slade as they headed for the Golconda.

"No, not luck," Slade differed. "I've revised my opinion of that. Not luck, but a mind that instantly sizes up a situation correctly. Like knocking the lamp over rather than taking time to shoot, and *taking* time to lock the back door behind him, thus foiling pursuit. He plans his every move with meticulous care. Evidently he familiarized himself with the layout of the store and knew just where to head for. The only real break he got was me slamming into the watchman when I started after him. That delayed me just the iota of time he needed to make good his getaway. He's in a class by himself. Wonder where in blazes he'll cut loose next?"

"Do you figure he left town right after he hightailed from the store?" Traynor asked.

"I'd hesitate to make any definite statement as to what he did or didn't do, or is going to do," Slade answered. "We may meet him coming around the next corner."

The sheriff instinctively dropped a hand to his gun butt and regarded the corner with suspicion. He looked a little sheepish when *El Halcon* chuckled.

"Just the same, I wouldn't put it past the sidewinder," he growled. "Well, here we are. Listen to the racket in there!"

The Golconda was indeed in an uproar. The watchman's doubtless somewhat garbled version of what happened in the store had apparently set everybody by the ears. Shouts of welcome greeted the entrance of the two peace officers, and it was some time before they were left to enjoy their drinks in peace.

After one snort, Slade settled for coffee. Then, with a few comforting words to Mary, he joined Black Pete at the madhouse usually known as a bar. For now business was really booming and all present appeared activated by a desire to get drunk as thoroughly and as quickly as possible. However, everybody seemed to be in a good temper and aside from a few isolated wrangles that were quickly suppressed, there was no trouble building up, so far as Slade could see.

"Well, how do you like the liquor business, Mr. Slade?" Pete asked, with his white smile.

"It is not without a certain quaintness and charm of its own, but I fear it is one that will quickly pall, so far as I'm concerned," Slade replied.

"If you could run it on horseback, I've a notion you'd like it better," Pete chuckled.

"You may have something there," Slade conceded. "Would be novel, at least."

"There's Clyde yelping for more stock," said Pete. "At this rate, we'll be cleaned out before daylight."

"Better a full safe and empty shelves than the reverse," Slade said. "Go ahead, I'll take over here."

The night wore on, wild, tumultuous, filled with uncouth sound. Drunken men staggered along the streets. The shrill voices of women added to the turmoil. The tired bartenders knocked the necks off bottles,

146

not taking time to pull corks, and gushed raw whiskey over the splinters, and nobody cared. Payday night in a frontier town! The scene was unreal, livid, medieval. Like to a dance of Apaches on the warpath, a dance of cliffdwellers under the moon's orb.

But tired nature was taking toll. Gradually, the weary revelers staggered to their rest. The windows glowed sickly against the advance of the dawn. Now the streets were gray. Lights winked out. Doors clanged shut. Bars and locks rattled. The east brightened, flushed with rose and scarlet that deepened to crimson and gold. The sun rose, casting its beams over the glitter of the desert, over the quiet beauty of the rangeland, rimming the mountain crests with saffron flame. A sweet breeze soughed up from the south, shaking a myriad glittering dew gems from the grass heads. Birds sang their homage to the glory of the day. But Gato slept!

13

"It was a wild, wild night, but I loved it," Mary Merril said to Slade as they dawdled over a late breakfast. "That is, after you were safe inside where I could keep an eye on you."

"Not a bad night, though," Slade answered. "Aside from the one incident, which worked out fairly well, a few skinned heads and bloody noses were the extent of the casualties. Everybody had a good time and behaved themselves fairly well; the sheriff's special deputies didn't find much to do."

Mary laughed. "Mr. Standish grew quite gay after a few drinks," she observed. "He and I had a little business talk, so for me it was also a profitable night."

Slade shook his head. "Yes, you always seem to come out on top." he said.

Mary smiled again, and the color in her cheeks brightened a little.

"Not always, dear," she said demurely.

Sheriff Traynor rolled in, looking somewhat the worse for wear.

"Coffee, black, and keep it coming," he told the waiter, and glowered enviously at Slade and Mary.

"Eating your breakfast as if you'd just come in from a nice ride," he grumbled. "Me, I couldn't touch a bite."

"I was too busy to drink much, and Mary never does," Slade explained. The sheriff grunted, and didn't look favorably impressed.

Black Pete was also quite chipper. "Best night we ever had," he said when he paused a moment to say good morning.

"I don't know how you do it," the sheriff sighed to Slade. "Folks who used to not want to stand beside Pete because he is black now go up and insist he have a drink with them. No, I don't know how you do it."

"By setting an example, perhaps," Slade replied. "There is plenty of good in most people, and it shows up, especially after they get rid of their silly prejudices. I'm very glad to see Pete doing so well. I learned he has an old father and mother back in Virginia who weren't doing so well until he started sending them money."

Mary Merril quoted softly from Robert Burns:

" 'And a man's a man for a' that!' "

"Exactly," Slade said.

And in his secret hide-a-way far to the south, Red Mike Talco paced the floor with nervous steps. In his eyes was an expression his followers, what was left of them, had never seen there before. Was it — fear?

"We've got to get rid of that big hellion," he said, his soft voice taking on a querulous note.

"You might have last night, if you'd shot it out with him," observed one of his men.

"Yes, if I hadn't seen what you stupidly did not, that watchman diving for his scatter gun as I knocked the lamp over," Talco replied. "If he'd gotten it in time, neither you nor I would be here. Now stop your gabbing and try and think of something."

A little later, the mill chimneys were again belching smoke. The workers, a trifle bleary-eyed but cheerful, their faces ashine with pleasant memories, were going about their chores blithely, chuckling over various happenings of the night before. While in the Gato General Store, Clifton Standish, the manager, was tabulating the contents of his safe, and preparing to ship it to the Alpine bank. Gato was back to normal.

In the Golconda, Sheriff Traynor started discussing Mike Talco.

" 'Cording to what Pedro's friends said, the hellion has a hang-out somewhere to the south of here," he remarked. "If we could just find that hide-out and drop a loop on the hellion there —"

"And what would you charge him with?" Slade interrupted.

"Why — why, attempted armed robbery, for one thing," said the sheriff.

150

"Did you ever see him commit a robbery, or attempt to commit one?" Slade parried.

"Guess I never did," the sheriff admitted. "But how about last night? You saw him, and Standish saw him, and Milt, the watchman saw him."

"Yes, and you'll recall that Standish and Milt could give only the vaguest description of the man who kidnapped Standish and did the talking," Slade countered. "He had his hat brim pulled down to his eyes, his neckerchief looped up to his mouth, and the light was not good. An able lawyer could quickly force them to concede that they could not identify the man as Talco, or anybody else they ever saw."

"But how about you?" protested Traynor. "You got a look at him."

"I got the merest glimpse of him," Slade replied. "I am convinced in my own mind that the man was Talco, but I am forced to admit, so far as practical identification purposes are concerned, I base my conviction on the fact that the man I considered to be Talco appeared to have red hair. Take that into court and see what happens to it. From his reactions, his mode of operation, and his planning, I 'know' it was Talco, but I couldn't prove it, not to the satisfaction of a judge and jury. We've got to get something more definite on him than we have now, and you might as well reconcile yourself to that."

The sheriff swore wearily, under his mustache, in deference to the presence of a lady. Mary giggled.

"I'm afraid I cramp your style, Uncle Chet," she said. "Uncle John is not so considerate. Every now and then he cuts loose with one that would make your hair curl."

"Reckon that's why yours is curly all the time, eh?" the sheriff retorted. "But really that hellion is enough to aggravate a saint. The Scriptures tell us Job was a patient man and never cut loose with cuss words, but if he'd had to put up with Mike Talco, he'd have swore the shingles off a barn."

Both his hearers laughed heartily. The sheriff did not appear to see any humor in the situation. He growled, and ordered a snort.

"That helped," he said after he'd downed it. "Now I believe I can eat a bite."

He did manage to put away a pretty fair surrounding and after another drink appeared to feel somewhat better.

"Was just thinking that our *amigo* Talco is pawing the ceiling about now," he remarked contemplatively as he loaded his black pipe with blacker tobacco. "One setback after another, and he ain't had a chance to peg a man over an ant hill or crucify him on the spines of a chola cactus for quite a while. Must be feeling sorta low."

Mary shuddered. "He's terrible," she said. "It frightens me even to think about him."

"He'll make a nice carcass," Traynor predicted cheerfully. "So don't worry about him; his time is coming."

"I hope so," she sighed. "But I can't keep from worrying."

"A female ain't happy unless she's worrying about some man," grunted the sheriff. "Hello! Here comes Gord and Standish; don't seem too bad."

The two managers did appear fairly chipper after a tumultuous night.

"But I still get the shakes when I think of that devil's eyes when he looked at me," said Standish. "There was frozen murder in them. Right then I wouldn't have given a plugged peso for my life."

"Oh, chances are he was in a killing mood, all right," replied Traynor. "And more so today."

"And I can't thank Slade enough for showing up when he did," said Standish.

"Did come in sorta handy," agreed Traynor.

"What you thinking about, Walt?" he

asked suddenly.

"I was thinking," Slade answered, "that our friend Talco must be running somewhat short of money, of which he needs plenty, to hold his men in line and keep things stirred up along the Border."

"Meaning that he's likely to hit some place soon?"

"So I presume," Slade replied.

"But where, how?" wondered Traynor.

"I don't know for sure," Slade admitted, "but I'm getting a hazy notion. I understand he's done quite a bit of cow stealing."

"That's right," nodded the sheriff. "From the spreads to the south and west of here. They've been losing plenty of stock and figure Talco is responsible."

"Very likely he is," Slade said. "That means he has a ready market south of the Rio Grande. And cows are a quick turnover, with the buyers always ready to pay cash on the barrel head for anything delivered to them on the south bank of the river. And right now the river isn't hard to ford. There's one place in particular I know of, east of Helena Canyon and not far from Castolon, which has always been a favorite with rustlers. Somehow, I keep thinking of that."

Sheriff Traynor nodded his understanding. He knew that few men were as familiar with all the peculiarities of the Big Bend as was *El Halcon,* in which respect he was truly *"El Halcon,"* the great hawk of the mountains, who sees all, knows all, and is ever ready to take advantage of opportunity.

"And you figure we might set a trap for the sidewinder there?" he asked.

"Frankly, I don't know, but I do believe it is worth trying," Slade answered. "We have nothing to lose, so far as I can see, and I can't think of anything else."

"One of your hunches, eh?"

"You may call it that, if you wish," Slade smiled.

"And they usually pay off," said Traynor. "Suppose we play it."

"A notion," Slade conceded. "We should have one more man with us, though," he added thoughtfully. "So the odds won't be too lopsided."

"Listen," Standish broke in. "My night watchman, Milt Evers, would sure like a chance at those devils; he's been fuming about what happened last night. Yes, nothing would suit him better than to go with you. I'll be glad to lend him to you, and as you know, he was once a Sieber scout and is thoroughly familiar with all the dodges of cattle thieves."

"That will be fine," Slade applauded. "Thanks, very much, for the offer; we're glad to accept it."

"I'll get in touch with him soon as he comes to work," Standish promised.

"We wouldn't leave town till after dark — less chance of attracting attention that way," Slade said.

"Here we go again!" sighed Mary. "Why the dickens couldn't I be a man, so I could go along!"

"I'm darn glad you're not," Slade declared with a heartiness that caused the others to laugh, and Mary to blush.

Gato was quiet after darkness fell, or at least as quiet as the mining town ever managed to be, and the little posse, unnoticed, slipped out several hours before midnight. It consisted of Slade, the sheriff, Deputy Chumley, and old Milt Evers, the general store night watchman, who was exultant at being permitted to go along.

"Don't appear to be wearing a tail," Slade announced, after carefully scanning the back trail for some time. "We'll speed up a bit now, but not too much; got a better than forty-mile ride ahead of us. Doesn't matter if we don't reach the river until close to daylight. I don't think they'll pull anything tonight, and if they do, we are already too late. We'll make camp near the river and take it easy during the day, and be all set for them if they do happen to shove a herd south. Well, here goes, watch your step, and hold your breath if you feel like it; nobody'll blame you."

Just what he meant by that they would soon find out.

By way of an old, little-known and seldom-traveled trail he led them. Through darksome canyons where the echoes of their horses' irons reverberated hollowly and ended in sighs and whispers of sound. Along precipitous slopes, past glowering crags. Along narrow edges of chasms where under their very elbows, white water foamed and thundered a thousand feet below.

"Bad enough in the daytime, but at night! Jumpin' blue blazes!" growled the sheriff. "If a feller happened to slip, he'd starve to death 'fore he hit bottom. Come to think of it, I've heard that birds sometimes fly into Santa Helena Canyon and starve to death there."

"That's right," Slade said, "Can't fly back out because of the down draft. This isn't quite that bad."

"Bad enough!" snorted Traynor. "Sure hope we don't hit anything worse."

"Not unless we find a rock fall has blocked

this snake track," Slade replied, adding cheerfully, "Of course there's always a chance that the vibrations set up by our horses' hoofs might bring down a slide, with us beneath it."

"Oh, Lord!" gulped Chumley. "I wish I'd led a better life!"

Slade laughed, and quickened the pace a little.

It was a cold, bleak pre-morning and the mist was rolling in dense clouds through the gorges when they neared the river. Above loomed huge pinnacles of rock. High above the dense haze, unseen from below, towered a dizzy peak with the pink glow of daybreak upon its lofty crest. The ground was wet, the rocks dripping, the grass covered with beads of moisture.

But in a sheltered gully ringed around by chaparral, the posse was snug enough. Ample provisions had been brought along in the saddle pouches and Slade had kindled a small fire of dry wood, confident that the thin stream of smoke would not be detected in the mist, if there was anybody to detect, which he thought unlikely. Bacon and eggs sizzled, coffee bubbled, and the men crouched around the fire made a satisfying breakfast. The horses did all right on a helping of oats topped off with grass.

With the first light, Slade scouted their position. Less than half a mile distant was the river, with the old trail running straight to the north bank. From shore to shore was the ripple that marked the position of the ford, easy enough for cattle to negotiate. He noted with satisfaction that dense thickets on either hand provided concealment for the posse.

"If Talco knows the Bend like I believe he does, he won't have to drive the cows through the bad country we traversed in the course of our short cut," he told his companions. "He can strike this trail where it levels off a half-dozen miles back and the going is good. That's the way I figure he'll work it if he grabs off a herd either to the east or west. Been done that way before. Of course I may be totally wrong in thinking he will rustle a herd, but somehow I don't believe I am."

"Chances are you ain't," said Traynor. "And we'll be all set for the devils if they come ambling along this way. Now what?"

"Now we take it easy," Slade replied. "We've got a lot of time before us and might as well put it to good use."

They did, mostly in sleep.

14

At dusk they cooked another meal and ate. Then, after a smoke, prepared for business.

"We'll get set shortly after full dark," Slade said. "For there's always the chance that they staged a raid last night, not long before dawn, when everybody sleeps the soundest, and holed up the cows somewhere in the hills. Easy enough for somebody thoroughly familiar with the section. There are old trails everywhere through the hills, some of them so stoney and shadowy that it is practically impossible to track a herd by way of them. If so they might start for the river as soon as it is dark, so we'll take no chances."

"Any other way by which they could cross the river?" Traynor asked.

"Yes, there is," Slade replied. "Remember that fork we passed a little more than a mile to the north? That fork leads to another ford, one seldom used, for it is not as good as this one, although it could be negotiated with the river as low as it is now. However, I can't see any reason why they should choose that one. Here is the logical crossing, where the buyers will wait."

After dousing the fire they made their preparations, which were simple. They took up their post on the river bank, in the growth close to the trail, with the horses tethered handily.

"Now all we can do is wait," Slade said. "Sure you can smoke, only cup the matches against the unlikely chance that somebody might be watching on the far side of the river."

"Everything going smooth so far," commented the sheriff as he lighted up.

"Yes," Slade agreed, "but somehow I have a feeling everything is going too darn smoothly. Why? I don't know, I just feel that way."

"I know how you feel," said old Milt Evers, the former Sieber scout. "Got that way sometimes myself, back in the old days. Feller gets suspicious of things when they seem ambling along like clock work."

"Exactly," Slade said. "Well, we'll see."

Overhead, the stars bloomed in beauty. The river was a broad band of silver-dimpled jet. The growth on the far bank a solid block of shadow. Only the moan and mutter of the stream chafing its banks broke the great silence of the wastelands, eerie, weird, seeming to voice a wordless threat. Or at least to Walt Slade's vivid imagination as stronger and stronger grew the premonition of evil, of something not as it should be.

A long and tedious wait followed, with the great clock in the sky wheeling westward. The wait that crawls along on leaden feet, hard on the nerves.

Suddenly Slade raised his head in an attitude of listening. To his amazingly keen ears had come a sound, an alien sound, the bawl, thin with distance, of a weary and disgusted cow.

"They're coming," he said to his companions. "Get — what in blazes!"

The remark was shot from him on wings of surprise and was echoed by puzzled mutters on the part of the others.

From the black block of growth on the south bank of the river four horsemen had emerged. They put their mounts to the water and sloshed steadily for the Texas shore. A few more minutes and they reached the bank and thudded past the astonished posse.

"What in the jumpin' blue Pete!" breathed Traynor.

"I don't know, but I'm pretty sure it's trouble of some sort," Slade whispered back. "And one thing I am sure of — I've been nicely outsmarted. Listen, now."

The sound of the hoofbeats dimmed, but the protests of the cattle loudened. Then abruptly another sound shattered the stillness, a grim, terrible, deadly sound, the sustained crackle of gunfire as shot after shot was fired.

As abruptly as it began, it ceased, and only the querulous complaints of the cattle broke the hush that had descended again like a fog blanket.

"My God! what *does* it mean?" gasped the sheriff.

"It means, I would say, that Red Mike has glutted his blood lust," Slade replied quietly. "That was the buyers being mowed down. I think I understand, now. Listen a few moments longer."

Every sense at hair-trigger alertness, the posse stood, straining their ears.

"The racket the cows are kicking up doesn't seem so loud, now," the sheriff said.

"Yes, just as I thought," Slade answered. "They've turned them into that side track and are heading for the other crossing I mentioned, three miles to the east, where there'll be another bunch of buyers, hellions of their own caliber, the chances are. Somehow, Talco inveigled the first bunch of buyers to cross the river to receive the cows. They were murdered and robbed of the money they packed to pay for the stock. All right, fork your broncs and let's go; we want to catch up with the devils before they join

163

forces with the second bunch of buyers. Steady, though, we don't want to run into a trap."

He set the pace, fairly fast, and they rode north on the old trail. They had covered somewhat less than a mile when the starlight showed four riderless horses standing patiently by the side of the trail. And sprawled in the dust were four motionless forms.

"Don't stop," Slade said. "Nothing we can do for those poor devils. All right, into the sidetrack and speed up. Hear the cows? Not too far ahead."

At a fast pace, they spurred along the side track. The ground was hard and stoney and the horses' irons clanged loudly.

"They'll hear us coming, but not too soon, I figure," Slade said. "Shoot to kill; we can't expect any mercy if they get the upper hand."

A moment later he exclaimed:

"There they are! Five of the sidewinders shoving the cows along."

He slid his high-power Winchester from the saddle boot as he spoke. Without drawing rein, they swooped down on the dark mass that was the moving herd. Slade could just make out the white blur of faces as the outlaws turned in their saddles.

"They've heard us!" he said. "Look out!"

164

From the ranks of the outlaws flame gushed. A bullet sang past, not too close. Slade's voice rang out:

"Trail, Shadow, trail!"

The great black horse lunged forward, the posse thundering at his heels but quickly losing ground.

With slugs buzzing around him like angry hornets, Slade estimated the distance. A bullet ripped his sleeve, another touched the brim of his hat. Again his voice sounded, "Easy, Shadow, easy!"

Instantly Shadow leveled off to a smooth running walk. Slade clamped the Winchester to his shoulder. The rifle gushed fire and smoke. And back of that flaming muzzle were the eyes of *El Halcon*.

A rider whirled from his saddle to lie prone in the dust. Slade shifted his rifle muzzle a trifle, his eyes glanced along the sights; he squeezed the trigger.

A second saddle was emptied. A voice roared a command and the three remaining horsemen scudded around the moving herd and raced east. The posse whooped with triumph.

"Don't follow them," Slade shouted. "No telling where they're scheduled to meet those other devils and we might find ourselves hopelessly outnumbered. Turn the cows, fast, and get them headed back to the main trail. Never mind those bodies; we haven't any time to fool with them."

The experienced cowmen quickly accomplished the maneuver. The bewildered cattle, bellowing protest, streamed back the way they had come.

"We've got to make it to where the trail narrows between the slopes, and in a hurry," Slade told the others. "I've a feeling the hellions will be after us before long. Once we are between the slopes I have no fear of an attack from the rear, but out here in the open we could be surrounded."

While his companions shoved the herd along, Slade rode drag some little distance behind the rearmost cows, constantly glancing over his shoulder, anxiously, for they had some distance to go before reaching comparative safety. Abruptly he uttered an exclamation. Far behind, clearly seen, by his eyes, in the starlight, seven or eight riders had materialized, speeding their horses.

But there was no making good time with the weary cows and the distance quickly shrank.

"Keep going," Slade shouted, glancing ahead to where the trail ran between the precipitous slopes not too far off. He pulled Shadow to a halt and faced the pursuit, the high-power Winchester ready.

Now the pursuers were firing volley after volley, but the range was too great for anything but an exceedingly lucky shot. Slade waited another moment, still another. The bullets were coming closer, but for a third moment he held his fire; he wouldn't have time to make up for a couple of misses.

Up came the rifle. It steadied. The report rang out like thunder. And an outlaw fell.

Again that slight shift of the muzzle. Again the icy gray eyes glancing along the sights. And the pursuit was short two.

That was enough. They jerked their horses to a halt and fired as fast as they could pull triggers, without results. Slade turned Shadow and jogged along behind the herd.

"Think they've got enough?" Traynor shouted as *El Halcon* drew near.

"They have," Slade replied. "They know we could finish them all off before they could get close enough to inflict damage. And right ahead are the slopes, where they can't circle around us, their only chance."

The sheriff heaved a sigh of heartfelt relief as the slopes closed in and the track narrowed.

"Thank Pete for your eyes and that gun of yours," he said prayerfully. "Well, we didn't do so bad, after all. Got the cows back and

167

did for four of the wind spiders, I believe it was. That was a heck of a sight better than I figured at one time."

"I see those critters are wearing a Tumbling-R burn," Slade remarked. "You happen to know where that spread is located?"

"Yep," Traynor replied. "It's old Calvin Radwell's holding, in a valley about eight or nine miles to the northeast of here, so far as I can judge."

"I think I know a side track that will lead us to it," Slade said. "Just beyond the next canyon that bends to the east. Yes, I'm sure I do. We might as well run them back where they belong."

"That's a notion," the sheriff agreed. "We can tie onto a surrounding there, of which I'm feeling the need, and the pouches are plumb empty of grub. Didn't happen to notice, did you, if Talco was one of those you downed?"

"I'm confident he wasn't," Slade replied; "the way things were handled, I figure he was still in charge. Well, he gratified his killer instinct and I expect he lifted a hefty sum from those poor devils of buyers. I expect he figures *he* didn't do too bad."

"The blankety-blank!" growled Traynor. "Wonder how he got the buyers to meet him

168

on this side of the river?"

"Hard to tell,' Slade replied. "Evidently he is a very smooth talker. He may have told them he didn't wish to approach the river for fear of being recognized as a cow thief by some of the dupes who look upon him as a *liberator.*"

"Yep, that could be it," the sheriff conceded. "What about all those carcasses scattered around?"

"Well, we're in Brewster County, your bailiwick, so you can do whatever you see fit," Slade answered.

"I'll see," said Traynor. "May get Radwell to lend me some of his boys to pack 'em in. Figure he'll be glad to, after getting his cows back, nearly a hundred head, I calc'late. Anyhow, the horses they rode will need looking after. That is if the bunch didn't round 'em up — valuable critters."

"Possibly they did," Slade said. "If they didn't, somebody else will sooner or later. Expect Radwell will be glad to have them."

"That's a notion, too," the sheriff agreed. "I'll put it up to him."

With the wornout cattle, progress was very slow and the sun was up before they reached the mountain-locked valley which, like many of its kind in the Big Bend, provided excellent pasture, and another hour had passed before they sighted the Tumbling-R *casa*.

An astounded and very grateful man was old Calvin Radwell when his stolen herd came into view.

"I was plumb sure they were gone for good," he said. "I'm sure beholden to you fellers; that many beefs run into a hefty passel of *dinero*."

He readily agreed to lend his hands, a full dozen in number, to assist in collecting the various bodies, if they were still where the posse left them, and to take care of the stray horses.

After a hearty breakfast, everybody lay down for a few hours of rest before further activity. It was early afternoon before they roused up and, after coffee and a snack, were ready for business.

"I'm heading back to town," Slade told the sheriff. "Guess you can make out all right."

"Sure," said Traynor, "Chumley and old Milt are going along, and I reckon we haven't anything to worry about. You go ahead and look after things in town. Be with you in the next couple of days. Yes, I know how to get out of here without following that blasted snake track of yours."

Slade rode steadily at a good pace through

the golden sunshine and the star-burned hours of darkness. He concluded things hadn't gone too bad, although he still felt he had been outsmarted, in a way. However, he found some consolation in the fact that it would have been impossible for anybody to foresee Talco's utterly unexpected move. The snake-blooded devil! Murder to him was in the nature of a pastime. At least, this time his victims had died swiftly and mercifully, without having to undergo fiendish tortures.

Well, Red Mike had escaped once more, but perhaps his luck would run out sometime. Slade was grimly determined to make it run out, were that humanly possible.

It was past midnight when he reached Gato. After caring for his horse, he headed for the Golconda, where he found Mary Merril and Black Pete anxiously awaiting him, the girl with a nice case of the jitters developing. There also were Dick Gord and Clifton Standish.

"We just couldn't sleep until we learned something," the Contention manager explained.

"Everybody fine as frog hair," Slade replied, and gave them a brief summary of the stirring events since leaving Gato.

"We'll get the real story from Sheriff

171

Traynor," Mary said. "Just got all the lucky breaks again, the way you tell it. Anyhow, you're back safe and that's all that really counts."

The others voiced emphatic agreement. Pedro, the cook, delivered, in person, a surrounding fitting to the occasion.

"And now I think we'd all better call it a night," Slade said. To which nobody objected.

15

When Slade descended in search of breakfast around noon, he thought the Golconda rather active for a week day. There were quite a number of miners present, more than those of the night shift that usually showed up for a short period, later in the day. Black Pete had an explanation.

"The Contention Mine is shut down for the day," Pete said. "They are doing some work in the engine room, I heard."

After breakfast, Mary not having put in an appearance, Slade went for a walk. As he strolled about the town, he gradually developed a feeling that he was constantly under surveillance. He saw nothing, heard nothing he considered suspicious, but the conviction grew that somebody was keeping tabs on his every move.

Well, that was not altogether unexpected. Had happened before. Aside from being a little more alert than ordinarily, he gave it little thought.

When he returned to the Golconda, he found Mary at her breakfast, with Dick Gord keeping her company. The manager verified Black Pete's explanation of the closed mine.

"Yes, had to do a little work on the winning gear," Gord said. "All finished now, but not much sense in sending the boys down for only a couple of hours or so. Let 'em take it easy for the rest of the day.

"And by the way, your tip you gave me concerning the drainage system sure paid off. Working perfectly, now. How'd you like to take a look at it? As I said, the mine's shut down for the day, but there is always somebody in the engine room to handle the cage and drop us down to the lowest level."

"Not a bad idea," Slade agreed. "Nothing else much to do, so far as I can see."

"Fine!" said Gord. "Just a little over a mile to the southwest to the mine. We'll tie onto our horses and jog down there."

"And try and keep him out of trouble for a change," Mary begged.

"Don't see how he can get into trouble at

173

the mine," Gord returned cheerfully. "That is unless the mountain takes a notion to squat down on us, which I consider unlikely. All set, Walt?"

It was but a short jaunt to the mine, where the horses were stabled with the mine mules. There was nobody around the pit head except the man in charge of the engine room. He greeted Gord cordially — the manager was popular with his men — and Slade with respect.

"We're going down to the lowest level, Steve," Gord told him. "You can pull the cage back up and we'll signal when we want it — don't know how long we'll be down."

"Certainly, Mr. Gord," the engineer replied, and manned his levers.

"Yes, that double sump arrangement you advocated, which allows the sediment to settle, works fine," Gord remarked to *El Halcon*. "Thanks to you, we haven't been bothered by plugging since we installed it, and the flow is much better and easier to control. Well, here we are, and down we go."

The Contention was a shaft mine and a deep one. They entered the cage, a small railinged platform, and shot down and down and down to the lowest level, where the cage came to a halt. Adjusting their cap lights, they stepped out into the tunnel.

The silence of the mine was oppressive, like to the silence of death, a vivid tangible thing. On the surface of the earth there is always some sound or motion, and though in itself it may be imperceptible, yet it does dull the sharp edge of absolute stillness.

But here in the dark depths of earth heart, there was none. They were cut off from the echoes of the living world as if they were truly dead.

Slade always experienced that feeling in the reaches of a mine. It was eerie, unreal, but somehow he found it restful. So, he imagined, must be the undisturbed silence of the grave.

Together he and the manager tramped slowly along the tunnel, with only their own small sounds for company, their voices hollow, muffled, their footsteps crowding close back against them. On work days there would be cheerful and animated sounds, with a winking sparkle of lights flitting hither and thither in and out among the intricate maze of tunnels and drifts, but today there was only silence, and abysmal darkness.

But gradually they realized there was a tiny and soft sound, all but blanketed by the dead weight of the silence, the faint gurgle of water in the ditches, on its way to the double sump, for the Contention was a fairly wet mine.

Over their heads towered a vast web of interlocking timbers that held the walls of the gutted lode apart. The timbers were eighteen inches square. First one of the great beams was laid on the floor, then upright ones, five feet high, were stood upon it, supporting another horizontal beam, and so on, square above square, like the framework of a window. Up and up into the gloom, for nigh a thousand feet.

As they walked, Gord pointed out salient features dealing with the changes embodied in Slade's plan, including a piping system which expedited the flow of water from upper drifts. *El Halcon* found it all of interest.

The gallery seemed endless, but eventually they reached the far end wall, and after pausing for a comfortable smoke, retraced their steps.

They were trudging along in silence at a point where the gallery curved gently, and no great distance from where the shaft led to the open air, when Slade suddenly halted, his head cocked in an attitude of listening. Gord glanced at him inquiringly.

"Hold it, and keep your voice low," Slade breathed. "The cage just came down; I wonder why?"

176

"Perhaps somebody wants to see me about something," Gord whispered in reply. Slade nodded, and listened a moment longer.

"No footsteps, no voices," he muttered. "Somebody 'pears anxious to keep quiet.

"Extinguish your light," he added, dousing his own. "Now ease ahead a little, quietly."

A few slow steps, and Slade's ears caught a sound that came from the darkness just around the curve, a tiny slithering sound, as if someone were endeavoring to tread softly on the rock floor.

"Hold it!" he breathed.

And at that instant, Gord's forward reaching foot struck a fragment of stone and sent it clattering along the rock floor.

From the darkness ahead came a startled exclamation. Slade went sideways, hurling Gord from him in the same ripple of movement.

A gun blazed, only a few yards distant. Gord gave a gasping cry. Slade drew and shot with both hands as fast as he could squeeze trigger, the drum roll of reports sending a riot of echoes bouncing back and forth among the timbers above.

There was a scream, that crescendoed to a bubbling shriek and chopped off short. Slade weaved and ducked and slithered as flame gushed from the darkness. He fired again, left and right. A cry knifed through the booming reports, a thud, then a low moaning that quickly stilled.

Tense, alert, *El Halcon* stood listening. Reaching far out, he rapped sharply on a timber with his gun barrel, and instantly changed position. Nothing happened. Taking a chance, he holstered one gun, fumbled a match and, holding it well away from him, struck it.

The tiny flicker of flame showed Gord sagging against a timber, looking dazed, and two motionless forms sprawled on the floor.

"Guess that takes care of that," Slade remarked, touching a second match to his cap light. "You hurt much, Dick?"

"Slug just barely touched my head," the manager replied, rubbing it vigorously. "What on earth does it mean?'

"I thought I was being watched in town," Slade said. "Evidently I was. We were followed to the mine and the devils either knew or guessed we would be on this level, and set a nice little trap for us. If we'd gone bulging ahead with our lamps lighted, we'd very likely gotten blown from beneath our caps."

"And we would have for sure if you hadn't heard the cage come down," declared Gord.

"Just as I would have caught one dead center if you hadn't taken time to shove me out of the way. I won't forget that, Walt. Now what?"

"Now top side as fast as we can get there," Slade answered. "I'm worried about your engineer. Never mind the bodies, leave them for the sheriff to take care of. Let's go! The cage operates from below, of course?"

"Right," Gord said.

Running at top speed, they quickly reached the cage. Slade sent it whizzing to the outer air and sped to the engine room.

The engineer lay near his controls, his head in a pool of blood that had flowed from a nasty gash just above his right temple.

Kneeling beside him, Slade felt of his pulse, explored the vicinity of the wound with sensitive fingertips.

"He's alive, and I don't think he's too badly hurt," he announced. "Stay with him, and don't let him move his head."

Racing to the stable, he secured his medicants from his saddle pouches and returned. Very quickly he had the wound smeared with antiseptic ointment, padded and bandaged, the flow of blood stopped.

Straightening up, Slade rolled a cigarette. "That should hold him until he sees the doctor," he said. "There's no fracture, so far as I can ascertain. I think he'll be coming out of it before long. Then maybe we can learn something."

A few minutes later, the injured man began muttering. He opened his eyes and stared blankly at Slade bending over him.

"How do you feel?" the Ranger asked.

"Not too bad," the other mumbled. "Sorta woozy, and my head hurts, but I'll make it."

"Sure you will," Slade said. "Think you can sit up?"

"Uh-huh," the engineer replied. With Slade's assistance, he did so, held his head in his hands a moment, then grinned wanly. Slade gently raised him to his feet, placed him in a chair, and rolled him a cigarette, on which he puffed gratefully. Slade waited until he had finished his smoke, then:

"Perhaps you can tell us what happened?" he suggested.

"Hardly know," the engineer answered, drawing in a lungful of steadying smoke. "Two fellers rode up. I'm pretty sure one of them worked here at the mine for a while. Said they wanted to see you, Mr. Gord. I told them you were down below. The one I believed worked here said it was urgent and they should see you right away, and asked me if I would send 'em down to where you were. Didn't see any reason why I shouldn't, so I turned around and reached for my levers. That's the last thing I remember, except a lot of stars and comets."

"Pistol whipped you from behind," Slade nodded. "Very smooth, nicely planned and executed, except for one little slip. The Talco touch. Lucky for you he wasn't along," he added to the engineer. "Chances were he'd have struck a bit harder, and you wouldn't be telling us about it."

"And," Gord broke in, "that little slip you mentioned was the slip of trying such a thing on *El Halcon.*"

"Possibly," Slade smiled, "but the slip I was thinking of was one of them scuffing his foot on the floor of the gallery; that gave the thing away." He glanced out the door.

"See there are a couple of saddled and bridled horses tethered to the rack over there," he said. "Good-looking critters. Hand them over to Steve here, to make up for his cracked head. He can sell them for enough to buy a drink or two.'

"I'll do that," Gord promised, "and help him unload 'em. Now what?"

Slade turned to the engineer. "Think we can leave you alone for a little while?" he asked. "The engines must not be left unattended."

"Sure," Steve replied, his voice back to normal. "I'm okay now. Much obliged for patchin' me up."

"Then we'll head for town," Slade decided. "We'll send you a relief right away, and the doctor."

"Never mind about the doctor," Steve said. "No sawbones could do a better job on me than you did. I'll ride one of my horses to town and see — a bartender."

"Which I expect will do him more good than a doctor," Gord chuckled as he and Slade headed for the stable and their mounts.

"Yes, he's young, and rugged," Slade agreed. "Takes more than a cut head to keep that sort down. How does *your* head feel?"

"Done forgot about it," Gord returned lightly. "After all, the darn thing barely touched me, hardly a drop of blood drawn. I saw a few of Steve's comets, but that was all."

"A Forty-five slug packs a husky wallop, even if it does barely touch you," Slade said.

16

When they reached the Golconda, Gord quickly singled out a man capable of handling the engines should need be, and dispatched him to relieve Steve, telling him the engineer was slightly hurt, not mentioning how he happened to be hurt.

"You can ride my horse and Steve can bring it back here," he added. "He'll be headed for here anyhow. Okay, Walt, I see Miss Merril is giving us a hard look, so we'd better join her."

They did. She bent a searching gaze on Slade, turned to Gord.

"Well, did you keep him out of trouble?" she asked.

"I'm afraid I'm a poor guardian," the manager admitted, and recounted what happened in the mine, the account losing nothing where Slade was concerned. She listened in silence until Gord paused.

"If he went to church, I suppose the roof would fall in, or something," she said.

"He wouldn't be under it," Gord replied cheerfully. "Worrying about him is just a waste of time."

"I suppose so," she conceded, resignedly. "But he's got me talking to myself."

"Just so you don't talk in your sleep," Slade said.

"I never talk without an audience," she retorted.

Slade grinned. Gord chuckled. Mary made a face at both of them.

A little later, Steve, the Contention engineer, arrived, and soon the bar was buzzing over *El Halcon's* latest exploit. Slade escaped on the pretext of looking after the horses, which he did. He whistled blithely as he personally gave Shadow a rubdown, a currying, and a brushing.

But just the same he gave thought to the dogged persistence of Red Mike Talco. There was not a shadow of doubt but that Talco had him marked for death, and he would never stop trying until he himself was eliminated. And eliminating Mike Talco promised to be a formidable chore.

However, Slade did not unduly bother his head about the matter. He had been marked for death before, and was still alive and kicking. After all, if your number isn't up, nobody could put it up. A casuistic philosophy, perhaps, but a comforting one. At least *El Halcon* thought so.

He tweaked Shadow's ear, and was rewarded by a baring of milk-white teeth, said so long to the stable keeper and returned to the Golconda and the plaudits of the crowd there, which he felt he could very well do without.

However, the drinks, the girls, and the games were of more lasting interest to the gathering and shortly he was left in peace with Gord and Mary.

"Well, how do you like being famous?" chuckled the manager.

"Fame and notoriety are all too often synonymous," Slade replied judiciously. "Only the most discerning can differentiate the one from the other, the line of demarcation frequently being a hairline."

"Guess you're right about that," conceded Gord. "Which only a very smart person is capable of realizing."

"Stop showering him with compliments," Mary put in. "He's insufferable as is."

"Really, I don't think I ever met a more unassuming man," Gord differed. "He's always belittling his accomplishments."

"He's too darn sure of himself," Mary replied morosely. "A girl never knows for certain just where she stands with him."

"Then don't stand," Gord advised cheerfully. "Let us drink!"

"You're a big help," she said, her color mounting. "Yes, I'll have one, too; I feel I need it."

The night and the following day passed peacefully. For which Mary, at least, was duly thankful. Just before dusk the sheriff, Chumley, and Milt Evers arrived.

"Everything taken care of," the sheriff told Slade. Carcasses stowed away, inquest held.

Everybody cleared of wrong doing. Coroner didn't consider it necessary for you to be present; had all the evidence he needed. Those poor devils of Mexican buyers were shot to pieces. That sidewinder must have kept on blazing away at them after they were on the ground. He's a caution to cats! How's everything here?"

He listened with absorbed interest to an account of the happenings in the Contention mine, muttering cuss words under his mustache.

"The hellion just nacherly don't give up," he growled. "Well, he hasn't had much luck so far, and I don't think he will have. Maybe he'll figure that way and clear out."

"Unlikely, I'd say," Slade replied. "He's not the pulling out kind."

"He'll end up wishing he had," Traynor predicted. "Well, I can stand a snort and a surrounding. See Chumley and Evers are helping hold the bar up. How are you, Mary? How are you, Mr. Gord? Quite a rousing time you had, eh?"

"I can do without another such," Gord declared fervently. "I fear I'm like Clifton Standish, not fitted for such things."

"You came through all right," Slade assured him. "Didn't turn a hair."

"But I've got some that's turned gray,"

Gord replied.

"You have my sympathy," said Mary.

The sheriff downed his snort and stowed away a hefty surrounding. Pushing back his empty plate, he filled his pipe and puffed contentedly.

"So you have a couple more carcasses to add to the collection, eh?" he observed. "I'll haul 'em up tomorrow, if the mine rats don't beat me to it.

"Had a pet rat once," he added reminiscently. "Educated feller working for me named him Socrates. Only Socrates turned out to be a lady rat, and all of a sudden I had a flock of little soc rats on my hands. They were sockdolagers, all right. Turned plumb owlhoot and took over the place. Chewed up my best pair of boots and made a nest in my Sunday hat. And when a cat came around, they rared up and dared him to do his darnedest."

This moving tale of erratic adventure was received with undeserved incredulity, the sheriff wearing an air of indignant innocence.

Slade sauntered to the bar for a word with some of the miners there. Several corroborated the belief of Steve, the engineer, that one of the slain outlaws had worked in the mine a while back.

"Funny sort of a jigger," one said. "I remember him well. Did his work but was all the time asking questions. Seem to want to know all about this business, how the metal was got outa the ore, how much the silver bricks weighed, how much they were worth, and things like that. Quit after a while and I never saw him again."

Leaving the miners, Slade made his way to the end of the bar to lend Black Pete a hand with the chores. Hodges, the former head dealer, and now head floor man, was circulating through the crowd and everything was in order.

Slade was in a thoughtful and somewhat puzzled mood. Why, he wondered, had the outlaw showed such an interest in the silver bricks. Surely Talco did not contemplate a raid on a shipment. The bricks were cast in hundred-pound weights for the express purpose of foiling gentlemen with share the wealth notions. A hundred-pound brick was too heavy and unwieldy a weight to stow in a saddle pouch or balance behind the pommel of a speeding horse; such a thing had never happened, so far as he had ever heard.

But Mike Talco was a most unpredictable quantity. Ridiculous though it seemed, there was a chance he might have evolved a plan to solve the problem. What that plan could possibly be, Slade had not the slightest idea. In fact, he rather doubted that Talco had any such notion in mind; didn't seem reasonable. But back came the question, why the interest shown by the fellow who had undoubtedly been one of Talco's followers? Slade shook his head, and for the time being cast the matter from his mind.

But the darn thing kept creeping back, and when he returned to his table, he asked Gord a question.

"Dick, when do you plan to make your next silver shipment to Alpine?"

"Day after tomorrow," Gord replied. "Say! You're not figuring something might happen to those bricks, are you? Plumb out of the question."

"How are the bricks conveyed to Alpine?" Slade countered.

"By a heavy, reinforced cart," Gord said. "And just in case, there's an armed guard on the driver's seat, and another following on horseback. So you see there's very little chance of anything happening to the bricks; just doesn't make sense."

Slade was inclined to agree, but just the same he was formulating a little plan of his own, one he felt might get results. With such an opponent as Mike Talco, he considered it unwise to neglect anything that might provide an opportunity to drop a loop on that slippery customer. He decided to keep his notion to himself. In which *El Halcon* made a mistake. A well-meaning move would toss his plans into a cocked hat, figuratively speaking.

Once again the night passed quietly and Slade was awake and down to breakfast before noon. There he found Gord already putting away a meal. The manager greeted him, and rubbed his hands together complacently.

"I'll have to admit that the discussion of the silver shipment last night left me a trifle bothered," he said. "So I figured I'd get a jump on any enterprising gentlemen with notions. Instead of waiting until tomorrow as planned, I headed the cart for Alpine this morning. Figured that would fool 'em."

"The devil you did!" Slade exclaimed.

"That's right," answered Gord. "Don't you think it was a good idea?"

"It could be," Slade conceded, noncommittally, and gave his order to the waiter.

Just the same, he was not exactly easy in his mind; he experienced a premonition that all was not well. Judging from past experience, it was reasonable to believe that Talco kept in constant touch with activities in Gato and would very likely hear of the

190

change in plans.

Well, there was nothing he could do about it. The cart had hours start, and if anything was due to happen, it very likely had already, or would soon.

The most disturbing element, from Slade's point of view, was the indubitable fact that Talco had many contacts south of the Rio Grande, and could count on full co-operation from those contacts. It seemed preposterous that an attempt would be made against the unwieldy cart, but Talco was Talco, anything could be expected from that shrewd and far-seeing devil.

There would be a ready market for the bricks, worth many thousands of dollars, a temptation to any outlaw bunch, could they figure a way to tie onto them. Slade finished his breakfast, rolled a cigarette and waited for Mary to appear.

Meanwhile, miles from Gato, the laden cart was rolling steadily north. The seat guard and the one following on horseback exchanged quips, the driver whistled melodiously. Sunshine and peace! Or so it seemed.

An old legend tells how the king's war horse lost a nail from its shoe. Because the nail was lost, the shoe was lost. Because the shoe was lost, a battle was lost. Because the battle was lost, a kingdom was lost. The moral? The importance of trifles.

A somewhat far-fetched parallel might be drawn anent the guard's horse, which had a happier ending in that it saved a man's life.

Anyhow, the mounted guard's horse lost a shoe nail, or a couple of them. As a result, the loosened shoe on its left forefoot began to rattle. With a few cheerful cuss words, the guard pulled to a halt.

"Go ahead," he called to the others. "I'll catch up with you soon as I fix this blankety-blank thing." The cart rolled on.

Riders usually made provisions against such accidents, so the guard rummaged in his saddle pouch, drew forth a hammer and a couple of nails, and went to work on the loose shoe. Experienced in such matters, it didn't take him long to make the contrary shoe secure. He mounted and continued on his way at a fast pace, expecting to catch up with the cart in short order.

He had just topped a rise when he sighted the cart lumbering through a brush grown area where a side track flowed up from the south to join the main trail. He started to descend the far sag.

Suddenly from the growth sounded a crackle of gunfire. The horrified guard saw his two companions topple from the cart seat to the ground. The firing continued for a moment. He started to spur to their aid, then reined in. Both, he well knew, were beyond human aid. He'd just get himself killed.

From the brush flanking the trail bulged half a dozen riders. The cart horses were seized and halted. The guard gulped in his throat as one of the raiders fired three deliberate shots at the motionless forms on the ground. Another dismounted, hitched his horse to the tail gate, and mounted the cart seat. The cart swerved into the south trail and vanished from sight. The guard whirled his mount and sent him racing back to Gato.

17

Slade and Sheriff Traynor were sitting in the office discussing the doings of Mike Talco when the guard jerked his foam splashed horse to a halt outside the door, flung himself from the hull and rushed in, gabbling his story of what had happened.

The sheriff swore. Slade stood up.

"Chet," he said, "this may be it. The guard escaping may have upset all their calculations. They can't make time with that clumsy and heavily laden cart. With good luck we may catch up with them before they reach the river, for which they will undoubtedly be heading. Let's go!"

"Please," begged the guard. "Please let me go with you. I'm itching for a chance at those murdering devils. Please, Sheriff. Only you'll have to get me a horse; mine's spent."

"Okay, we'll get you one," acceded Traynor. "Six of them, you say? With you and Chumley there'll be four of us, enough to take care of the blankety-blank-blanks, if we can catch 'em. Run over to the Golconda and fetch Chumley, he's eating. We'll tie onto a cayuse for you."

At a fast pace, Slade and the guard, mounted on a fresh horse, led the way north by west via the Alpine trail. The miles flowed back and after a while they reached the spot where the bodies of the murdered driver and the seat guard lay. Here they paused long enough to move the bodies to the side of the trail and fold the hands on the breast. Each had been shot several times.

"The Talco way," Slade observed. "He shows no mercy. Well, perhaps we'll have a chance to even the score a bit, before long. They have a head start but won't be able to make much speed; we may catch up with them."

Turning into the side track, they followed

the trail of the stolen cart, the tire marks of the heavily laden vehicle plain to the eyes of *El Halcon*. Slade rode watchful and alert, although he thought there was scant danger of running into a trap; but anything could be expected of Red Mike and he took no chances.

But the miles skipped back under the horses' irons, with nothing happening. Birds sang in the thickets, little animals went about their various business in the rustling, many-tinted growth.

Then abruptly, on rounding a sharp bend, they came to a spot where a trail flowed from the southeast to join the one they were following, which ran almost due south. Slade instantly called a halt.

The surface of the track was hard and stony, but at the forks was a stretch of fairly soft ground which extended for a few yards. Here was plain evidence that the cart had turned into it.

"Now where in blazes are they headed for?" the Ranger wondered. "Well, we'll find out; let's go!"

Even more watchful, he rode. For the unexpected move on the part of the outlaws puzzled him.

On and on, with nothing happening, no sign of anything inimical. They covered

195

several fast miles, nearly half a dozen, and then, with a disgusted exclamation, Slade drew rein again. Directly ahead, the growth had thinned greatly, and the surface of the trail was very soft.

"Now what?" Traynor asked.

"Outsmarted, that's all," Slade replied bitterly. "The cart ahead of us is empty, the tire marks on the soft ground show that clearly, don't much more than score the surface."

"But what in blazes did they do with the bricks, hide them in the brush?" the sheriff demanded.

"No," Slade replied, turning Shadow to face the way they had come. "I'd say, and I'm confident I'm right, that there was another vehicle waiting at the forks. The bricks were transferred to it and it headed south, leaving the empty cart to follow the side trail as a decoy. Worked, too. I fell for it very neatly. Talco never misses a bet. Let's go, I figure we still have a chance to catch them."

"Figure Talco was with them?" Traynor asked as they sped back to the south trail.

"Probably with the second vehicle," Slade answered. "I'm pretty sure he wasn't with the bunch that killed the driver and the seat guard."

"How do you figure that?" said the sheriff.

"If he had been, he would have realized that the horse guard had fallen back for some reason or other and would have been waiting for him to reappear, or would have sent a couple of his devils to take care of him. The others quite likely concluded that the guard hadn't accompanied the cart."

"Wouldn't be surprised if you're right," Traynor agreed.

A little later, they swerved into the trail that ran due south.

Slade rode recklessly now, for he had little further fear of a trap, although with Talco, anything was possible. The devil with it! He'd taken a chance. And anyhow, he was fairly confident that his unusually acute senses would spot danger ahead before they ran into it. He gave Shadow his head and let him choose his own gait, holding him back a bit in deference to the slower mounts of the others.

The sun dropped toward the horizon. Shadows began thickening in the growth. Taller and more rugged loomed the mountains. Rougher and more winding the trail, but always wide enough to accommodate a cart or a light wagon. From the infrequently seen tire tracks, Slade was inclined to think the latter was drawn by four horses. Anyway, it was traveling darn fast and still no sign of it. Slade began to experience an uneasy feeling that they were too late, that the Contention silver bricks were already south of the Rio Grande, and beyond recall. For now the river was close.

Around a sharp bend they raced, and before them, less than five hundred yards distant, was the turgid flood of the stately River of the Palms.

Sheriff Traynor let loose an exultant whoop. For at the water's edge stood the wagon, with six horsemen grouped around it. And, two men handling the sweeps, a flat-bottomed boat was just putting in to shore.

"Get 'em!" howled the sheriff.

"Trail, Shadow, trail!" shouted Slade.

Forward lunged the great horse, the other thundering behind him. From the ranks of the outlaws puffed smoke; slugs whined past. Slade estimated the distance, drew his Winchester from the saddle boot.

A little more! A little more, despite the death whispering past. His voice sounded again:

"Steady, Shadow!"

With the horse's smooth gait scarcely jolting him, he clamped the rifle to his shoulder, squeezed the trigger.

A scream echoed the booming report. A

man lurched sideways from his saddle. Slade shifted the rifle muzzle. Again the smoke shrouded report, and a second saddle was empty.

Now Traynor and the others were shooting, a crashing volley. Two more outlaws went down. The other two, taken utterly by surprise, unprepared, nevertheless fought back with desperate courage as the racing horses swooped down on them. Slade caught a glimpse of the huge form and red hair of Mike Talco, partially shielded by the wagon. He swung the Winchester around, but Talco dived headfirst into the boat, shoved it from the shore with a thrust of his powerful arms, and flopped to the bottom, where the two crewmen were already cowering. Slade's bullets drummed against the thick planks of the side. Then the current caught it and hurled it down stream at racehorse speed.

Slade caught a fleeting glimpse of Red Mike's face peering over the gunwale. Then it dropped out of sight.

With a disgusted oath, he began reloading his rifle, although there was nothing left to shoot at.

Talco had done it again!

"But we didn't do so bad," chortled the

sheriff. "Got the bricks back and cleaned out his whole bunch. Not bad at all."

Shoving the Winchester into the boot, after making sure there was nothing to fear from the outlaws strewn on the ground like sleeping men, Slade turned to his companions.

"Anybody hurt?" he asked.

Blood was dripping from Chumley's left hand; he had caught one in the arm. The guard was inspecting a ragged furrow that scored the calf of his right leg. Slade and the sheriff were untouched.

After an examination, Slade decided the wounds were not serious. However, with the medicants from his saddle pouches, he patched them up to stop the bleeding and rendered the pair more comfortable.

"Yes, I'll have to admit we came out of it very well," he said. "Surprise is always a big advantage; threw the devils off balance for a moment, and before they could recover, it was too late, so far as they were concerned. But Talco! That brain of his works like a machine. Realizing that if he tried to escape on horseback, we'd very likely ride him down, he took the only other course available, and the right one, which means the chase will have to go on."

"Well, the next time he pulls something,

I've a notion he'll have to do it alone," the sheriff predicted optimistically. Slade shook his head in disagreement.

"He'll have little trouble getting another bunch together, if he really needs one. I gather that up till lately, his raids were highly successful and remunerative, supplying his men with plenty of spending money. His successes will be remembered, his setbacks forgotten. That's the way of the owlhoot brand. And the Talco sort is hard to keep down. We'll hear from him, unpleasantly."

He glanced at the sun; the lower edge was dropping below the horizon, turned toward the wagon. The tired horses had hardly moved during the ruckus. The dead outlaws' mounts were nibbling grass on the upper bank.

"The critters will have to have a couple of hours rest, at least," he said. "So let's get the rigs off so they can graze in comfort. A helping of grass will tone them up. And we might as well get a fire going and cook something to eat. I'm feeling the need of it."

The cart guard glanced apprehensively down the river.

"Don't think there's any chance of that devil getting another bunch of sidewinders together and coming back looking for us?" he asked.

"Not him," Slade replied. "He's had enough to hold him for one day. He'll land somewhere on the south shore, where he can finagle a horse, and head for his hangout. Don't worry about him."

The chore of caring for the horses was quickly accomplished. Staple provisions were always packed in the saddle pouches and soon all hands partook of an appetizing meal. Chumley and the guard suffered little pain, thanks to Slade's ministrations, and were lively as crickets.

"Sure glad we managed to even the chore for poor Shrig and Monty," remarked the guard. "I feel a mite better about them."

"I sent word to Gord to have them fetched to town," the sheriff observed. "He'll take care of it. Now if I just had a snort, I'd be rarin' to go."

"You'll have one, about noon tomorrow," Slade predicted. "We've got a long drag ahead of us.

"Incidentally, Talco has one of his bunch left."

"Yes?"

"Yes, the fellow who drove the decoy cart into the side track. Abandoned it somewhere along the line and took to his horse, which was hitched to the tail gate. Perhaps headed to the hang-out, or to some rendezvous with his boss."

"That's right," replied Traynor. "I'd plumb forgot about him."

A couple of hours after sunset, Slade decided the horses had built up enough strength to hit the trail. Harness and rigs were gotten into place, the bodies draped across saddles. One fine animal had very likely been Talco's, Slade thought.

With the body laden horses linked behind the wagon, the unburdened cayuse bringing up the rear, the trip back to Gato began.

It was a long jog and a slow one and the sun was well up in the eastern sky when the grisly procession threaded its way through the excited streets of the mining town. The bodies were placed in the sheriff's office, where Mary Merril and Dick Gord were waiting; the horses were cared for. Gord took charge of the loaded wagon. The curious had to be satisfied, for the time being, with a very brief account of what happened, and the thoroughly wornout posse sought much-needed rest.

18

It was well past nightfall when Slade awakened. For a while he lay drowsily listening to the rising murmur of voices in the street below; Gato's night life was getting under way.

Conning over recent events, he felt things were not going too badly. Mike Talco was still to be run down, but he believed Talco was definitely *on* the run, after suffering one setback after another.

But he experienced a premonition that the slippery devil still had an ace up his sleeve that he would play at the opportune time. Well, that was okay; he'd welcome a showdown. Get it over with one way or another.

Before descending the stairs, he cleaned and oiled his guns, making sure they were in perfect order, smooth in their sheaths.

Apparently he was first up, for when he reached the saloon, none of the others were in evidence. So, after a talk with Black Pete, he enjoyed a leisurely breakfast, dinner, or what have you, by himself.

For which he was glad, as it gave him an opportunity to do some uninterrupted thinking. He was smoking a cigarette over a final cup of steaming coffee when the sheriff ambled in.

"Guess Chumley and the guard are still sleeping, or getting drunk somewhere," he observed as he sat down and beckoned a waiter. "I sent them to see the doctor before going to bed. He changed the bandages, said there was nothing else that needed attention, and told them to get the heck out and stop cluttering up his place. He's a character, old Doc."

"I knew him in Sanderson," Slade said. "Always on the move. Old as he is, he's still got itchy feet. Typical of the frontier practitioner, but he knows his business." The sheriff nodded agreement and ordered a drink and a surrounding.

"Here comes your gal," he said. "Darned if you don't look like you've been snoozing, too," he greeted Mary.

"Why not?" she retorted. "I certainly did very little last night, with both of you out gallivanting somewhere and getting into trouble."

"Wasn't any trouble," the sheriff differed cheerfully. "Everything worked out fine and dandy; couldn't have been better."

"From the masculine viewpoint, I suppose," she replied. "I'm hungry." Slade beckoned a waiter.

"I took quite a passel of *dinero* from those carcasses," the sheriff remarked. "Not so much as we used to, though. I've a notion *amigo* Talco is getting a mite short of change."

"Which means it will be urgent that he pull something soon," Slade said.

"Well, it won't be the silver bricks," chuckled Traynor. "Dick is sending along a half-dozen guards with that wagon tomorrow, all strung out and ready for anything. Incidentally, a good wagon and good horses, makes up for the cart and horses he lost."

"No, I don't think he'll make a try for the bricks again," Slade agreed.

Deputy Chumley and the Contention cart guard wobbled in, exactly the word to describe their entrance, looking as if they had paused someplace else on the way. They waved hands and headed for the bar. Soon they had a crowd around them.

"Now you'll catch it," the sheriff chortled. "They're spreading it on thick; everybody looking this way."

Slade did catch it, praise and congratulations, and was thankful when Traynor suggested they go open the office in case somebody might want to look at the bodies.

Wasn't much better at the office. There he received more plaudits from citizens prominent and otherwise. As for the bodies, it was a reaction that had become monotonous.

Several persons recalled seeing one or more of the outlaws on the streets, in the shops, or drinking at the bars, but had paid them no mind. That was not strange, with cowhands from the various spreads constantly visiting the town, and chuckline riders pausing.

"Not that it makes any great difference," Slade said. "We know whom to look for and whom his hellions happened to associate with doesn't mean much. The bodies of the cart driver and the guard are at the undertaker's parlor?"

"That's right," Traynor answered. "Gord will give them a decent burial, and try to locate any relatives they may have left. Dick's a good man."

"Don't come any better," Slade agreed. "Well, guess we've done all we can here. Suppose we go back to the Golconda and I'll give Pete a hand; quite a crowd there tonight."

"Suits me," said the sheriff. "Dance-floor gals are easier on the eyes than those carcasses. Let's go!"

The Golconda was lively, all right, and both Slade and Black Pete were kept busy for a while. Crane Hodges was competently handling the floor and everything going smoothly. So ultimately Slade found time to sit down and catch his breath.

Meanwhile, Dick Gord had arrived to join Mary and the sheriff. The manager was in a cheerful mood.

"I'm sure beholden to you, Walt," he said. "Those bricks run to a lot of money. Would have been a heavy loss and would have meant trouble with the stockholders. It took eastern capital to open the mine and folks who are not familiar with conditions here quickly grow impatient with such matters."

"Glad to have been able to lend a hand," Slade replied. "And we got a good deal of satisfaction from cleaning out that nest of varmints, or the majority of them. I don't think they'll try it again."

"We'll try and be ready for them if they do," Gord said. "As Chet doubtless told you, I'm tripling the guard tomorrow, and warning them not to clump together."

"A good notion," Slade agreed. "Strung out, they'll be much less vulnerable to attack. You're learning fast."

"I have to," chuckled Gord. "Can't expect to have you around all the time to bail me out."

The night passed quietly enough, everything considered. Slade slept late the following morning, and when he headed for breakfast, Pedro, the old cook, beckoned him to the kitchen, led the way to the little table in the corner, and poured coffee.

"*Capitan,*" he said, "trouble brews at the Border. Men gather; men arm. A whisper goes that the day of liberation draws nigh, that wrongs will be righted, the evil punished. *Si,* I fear great trouble is in store for the river lands, unless something is done. But my *amigos* watch and listen. As do the friends of he who leads the orchestra, to whom *Capitan* gave the knife. *Capitan* will learn what is planned, and *El Halcon* will act; of that I doubt not."

"I'll do my best," Slade promised. "Keep in touch, Pedro, and *gracias,* you help greatly."

The old cook bowed his white head and repeated what he had said before,

"To be able to help *El Halcon,* the good, the just, is the great honor."

After finishing coffee with Pedro, Slade went out to breakfast in a very thoughtful mood. Evidently Talco was at work among the river country dwellers, stirring up, organizing. Were he not stopped, the result would be rapine and bloodshed along the Border, providing ample opportunity for profit for Talco, suffering for the dupes that would follow him. Slade was determined to stop him. How? He had no idea — yet.

Of course the simplest method would be to eliminate Talco, but were past performances a criterion, eliminating Red Mike was far from simple.

He resolved to keep what Pedro told him to himself, for he felt that at the final showdown, he must play a lone hand, his only companion, the prestige of *El Halcon.*

And he hoped the showdown, one way or another, would come soon, for he was growing somewhat weary of the saloon business and the quicker he was freed of the responsibility, the better. In fact, he considered there was no longer any real need for him to be present. Black Pete was now a prime favorite with the customers and Crane Hodges was competent, ambitious, and was fast getting all the angles at his fingertips. Slade felt he had fulfilled his promise to the dying Ralph Marshal and his mind was at ease on that score.

And the ever-present urge to be on the move was growing imperative. The out-trail was whispering, the far horizons beckoning. "We must go, go, go away from here!"

Mary Merril, who joined him at breakfast, sensed it.

"Yes, before long you will be moving on," she said. "As soon as your work here is completed."

"Let's hope it will be completed soon," he replied. "Then perhaps we can have a few restful days." Mary sighed.

"Rest and *El Halcon* are strangers," she said.

Late that afternoon, Pedro again summoned Slade to the kitchen, and he appeared to be laboring under suppressed excitement.

"*Capitan,*" he said, without preamble, "tomorrow night there will be a gathering, at which Talco the accurst will speak. He will beguile those misguided ones with smooth words and lying promises, and blood will flow."

"Do you know where the gathering will be held?" Slade asked.

"My *amigo* Alfredo Guevara knows," Pedro answered. "He will lead *Capitan* there, if *Capitan* so desires."

"I do so desire," Slade replied.

"*Bueno!*" said Pedro. "Alfredo also knows many of those who will be present. When the dark comes down, he will visit me here. He will talk with *Capitan.*"

"Fine!" Slade returned. "Pedro, you are really a big, big help."

The old cook looked very pleased.

When Slade visited the kitchen again, shortly after nightfall, old Pedro had company. A sinewy, dark-faced, glitter-eyed young Yaqui-Mexican with the ever present long throwing knife at his belt, another in his boot top. He bowed low to *El Halcon.*

"Pedro tells me you know where the gathering will be held," Slade remarked when they were seated at the little table, with coffee for him and wine for Alfredo.

"*Si, Capitan,* a hidden spot known to but few and not far from the river."

"And you will guide me there?"

"*Si, Capitan,* it will be the great pleasure to do so."

Slade thought a moment, sipping his coffee, and estimating the distance they would have to cover, and the time it would take.

"Guess we should start out shortly before noon tomorrow," he said at length. "You have a horse, of course?"

"*Si,* I have the *caballo,*" Alfredo replied. "The one he is that is good."

"Then we're all set," Slade said. "I'd like to get there before Talco arrives, if possible."

"We will," Alfredo replied confidently.

Slade did not inform Sheriff Traynor of what he had in mind, for more than ever he was convinced he must play a lone hand, perhaps with the odds heavy against him; but that was the chance he had to take.

An hour before noon the following day,

he and Alfredo set out, heading south with a slight veering to the east, and soon were following a track that even Slade didn't know about, for it seemed to spring from nowhere, and doubtless ended the same way.

Past mountain peak and towering crag, the Mexican led. Along the edges of dizzy cliffs. Through gloomy canyons walled by perpendicular rock or steep slopes. Besides white water, threading his way through stands of chaparral that encroached on the trail. For this was an old, old track, perhaps beat out by the feet of men before the Indians, or even the Aztecs.

The sun sank, the sky flamed a glory of color, paled to steel-gray, deepened to blue-black spangled by a myriad of stars. And still Alfredo led on and on. They entered a narrow canyon walled by irregular cliffs, and Slade knew they could be no great distance from the river.

Abruptly the Mexican, who had been continually studying the cliffs to the east, drew rein.

"There, *Capitan,* is our path," he said, pointing upward. "A dizzy path and narrow, but safe, for men of long ago smoothed the surface."

Now there was a moon almost directly

213

overhead, and by its light Slade saw a narrow ledge sloping up a cliff to vanish beyond a shoulder of rock. Alfredo put his horse to it, followed by Shadow, who blew dubiously through his nose but carried on.

It was a dizzy path, but Slade quickly saw that Alfredo was right; the surface had been smoother, and probably widened, by the hand of man.

Up and up it wound, gradually becoming steeper, until Slade estimated they must be more than a thousand feet above the floor of the canyon. It turned a shoulder, leveled off and ended, or seemed to end, at a wall of black rock.

A few more paces, however, and he saw that the black rock was pierced by the equally black mouth of a cave or tunnel. Into this ominous opening Alfredo rode unhesitatingly.

Now the horses slowed their pace, blew nervously, and lifted their feet gingerly, for about them swirled a damp draft and from a tremendous depth came, faintly, the sound of rushing water. And Slade sensed that the track had narrowed.

However, Alfredo continued composedly, and after a bit, Slade saw light ahead that quickly strengthened. A little more and they rode out of the tunnel into the white flood of the moonlight. Before them was an almost circular amphitheater or bowl perhaps five hundred yards in diameter and walled by tall cliffs.

A single glance told Slade that it was nothing more nor less than the crater of a once active but long extinct volcano. And near the far side was a square building constructed of huge blocks of lava that had withstood the ravages of time. Slade recognized it to be an ancient Aztec temple, quite likely a temple to Quetzalcoatl, the great Aztec god of the air, whose temples were always, if possible, built in lofty places.

And through the paneless windows shone light.

19

Alfredo did not ride across the bowl to the temple, but followed its curving side until they were not far from the ancient building, from which came voices and an occasional laugh.

"This way is better," the Mexican murmured. "The brothers are there, I know, and although I do not believe the *cabron*, Talco, has yet arrived, it is best not to take chances. Here we will leave the *caballos;* the others are farther on."

"You are right," Slade agreed as they dismounted where a straggle of brush managed to subsist on the lava soil. He made sure that Shadow was pretty well concealed by the growth; the horse was outstanding and might be remembered by the sharp eyes of Talco, did he sight it.

For a long moment, Slade gazing at the old temple, recalling that horrible sacrifices were offered on the altar of Quetzalcoatl, and Red Mike Talco qualified as a disciple of the terrible god of the air, the heights, and the storm. He loosened his guns in their sheaths. He believed he could keep the situation under control. If he couldn't — well, Talco wouldn't have to worry about *him* any more. With a shrug of his broad shoulders he strode toward the wide door of the temple, Alfredo following close behind.

At the door, Slade did not hesitate, but stepped into the large and lofty-ceiled room, his tall form outlined against the moonlight.

Lounging about in comfortable positions, wearing an air of expectancy, were between thirty and forty men. A single, swift, all-embracing glance told him Talco was not of their number.

The patter of words ceased. The concentrated stare of eyes could almost be felt. Then a voice cried out:

El Halcon! It is El Halcon!"

"Aye, it is *El Halcon!"* Alfredo called. *"El Halcon!* the good, the just, the compassionate, the friend of all who know sorrow, or fear, or injustice! *El Halcon,* the friend of the lowly! Hear him, my brothers, hear him!"

"We will hear him," the voice called in reply.

Slade stepped forward, until he was close to the group, which had clumped together, and smiled, the flashing white smile of *El Halcon.* It was mirrored by answering grins in dark faces. His deep and musical voice rang out:

"Amigos, you are here on a fool's errand, misguided, betrayed by lying words. Listen! A day will come when a true *liberator* will arise, a man of the people, who will right wrongs, bring justice, fair dealing, and prosperity to a great land and a great people. But Red Mike Talco is not that man. He is but a Border thief with only his own selfish interests at heart. He will not lead you to victory. He will lead you to death!"

The great voice stilled, and *El Halcon* stood waiting. For another moment there was silence, while the words he spoke sank in. Then abruptly someone called:

"El Halcon speaks no lies!" There was a

217

spreading murmur of agreement.

And Walt Slade knew, come what might, they were his.

Outside sounded a beat of hoofs on the rock floor of the crater. Slade turned to face the door.

"Out of line!" he snapped over his shoulder. There was a quick scattering, leaving only him and Alfredo in line with the door.

The beat of hoofs ceased. There was a mutter of voices. Another moment, and two men stepped through the door, to pause, blinking at the light. Foremost was Red Mike Talco!

Slade's voice again rolled in thunder through the echoing room:

"In the name of the State of Texas, I arrest Mike Talco and others for robbery and murder! Anything you say —"

Talco yelled, a high-pitched, screeching yell. His face convulsed with maniacal fury, he went for his gun as did his companion. Firing with both hands, Slade answered the outlaws shot for shot. Alfredo's knife buzzed through the air and Talco's companion fell, screaming hoarsely, his throat transfixed by the long blade.

A slug grazed Slade's temple, hurling him sideways, blood flowing down his face. Another just grained his right arm. He recovered, squeezing both triggers. Talco rushed forward recklessly, firing at the weaving, ducking Ranger.

Abruptly he halted, as if struck by a mighty fist. Still, he stood erect, only on his contorted face was a look of horrified disbelief. The guns dropped from his hands. He leaned forward, and fell, slowly at first, then with a rush, like to a smitten tree of the forest, to lie writhing.

Holstering his Colts, Slade knelt beside the dying outlaw. Talco glared up at him with glazing, hate-filled eyes. He gasped words through the blood frothing his lips:

"Damn you! Damn you! You — take — over!"

Slade shook his head. "No, Talco," he said. "I do not take over. Justice and law and order take over."

From the cunningly concealed secret pocket in his broad leather belt he drew something that caught the light and cupped it in his hand, a gleaming silver star set on a silver circle.

The feared and honored badge of the Texas Rangers was the last thing Red Mike Talco saw on this earth.

Wearily, Slade straightened up, returning the star to its hiding place. For a moment he gazed down at the dead face, then turned

219

to the silent, awe-struck gathering. A voice called:

"The hand of *El Halcon* is sure!"

"And the blade of Alfredo is also sure," Slade called back. He turned to the young Mexican. "*Gracias, amigo,* were it not for you, things might have ended differently."

"It was an easy cast, in this good light," Alfredo replied cheerfully. He withdrew the knife from his dead foe's throat, wiped the blade on the fellow's shirt, and sheathed it.

The Mexicans gathered around the bodies, staring down at them in silence for a moment.

"The justice of *El Halcon,*" one said. "May *El Dios* grant it will ever prevail." He addressed Slade,

"*Capitan,* we were about to prepare food and eat. Will you honor us with your presence?"

"It is I who am honored," Slade replied.

The bodies were shoved aside and soon the room echoed to talk and laughter. Death lay beside the rock wall, but to the mercurial Mexicans that meant little. Already, Red Mike Talco was a finished story to be forgotten.

While the food was being prepared, Slade and Alfredo cared for their horses, and those ridden by the outlaws.

"We will need them to pack the bodies to town," Slade said.

A hearty meal was enjoyed by all. Then, after a smoke, the Mexicans arose, bowed low to *El Halcon,* murmured words of blessing, and departed. Their talk and laughter died away in the tunnel, and only the stars and the moonlight remained.

"The cayuses will need a few hours of rest, and I think we had better emulate their example," Slade told his companion.

Before lying down, Slade more thoroughly examined the interior of the temple. Against the far wall from where the fire was built stood a statue of the god. Scaled and feathered, winged and serpentine, it was indeed a frightful object. The nose was an exaggerated eagle beak, the mouth, wide, reptilian, cruelly pulled down at the corners.

Before the statue stood the stained and blackened altar on which sacrifices to the god underwent fiendish tortures, screaming for death to relieve them of their agonies. Quetzalcoatl, the terrible!

And in the flicker of the firelight, the obsidian eyes of the god seemed to move, their stony gaze turning toward where lay the bodies of Red Mike Talco and his henchman.

Slade breathed deeply and slowly retraced

his steps to where Alfredo waited. Quetzalcoatl had claimed his sacrifice!

Spreading their blankets near the dying fire, they were soon fast asleep.

With the first flush of dawn they set out on the long return trip to Gato. Walt Slade experienced a quiet content. He had come into a section plagued by prejudice, hate, and fear. He would be leaving behind him good fellowship, understanding, and peace. Ranger work! Yes, it was really worth while.

Darkness was falling when they reached Gato, where there was immediately rejoicing and relief over the elimination of the menace of Red Mike Talco. Mary and the sheriff and Dick Gord listened with absorbed interest to the account of the slaying of Talco and his one remaining follower. They insisted that Alfred do most of the talking, knowing very well they wouldn't get the half of the story from Slade.

"And that takes care of that," said Traynor. "Now maybe we will have a mite of peace for a change. That is, until some other sidewinder shows up."

"If one does, Walt will pop around the corner and take care of him for us," Gord predicted cheerfully. The sheriff nodded agreement.

"What next?" he asked of Slade.

"Next, I'm on my way," the Ranger replied. "I'm turning over my Golconda holdings to Crane Hodges. He and Pete are pulling well together and I figure they'll keep on that way. Chet, you can take care of any necessary legal angles. I'm riding to Sanderson with Mary, to spend a few days at her uncle's ranch. Then back to the Post to see what Captain Jim has lined up for me. Be seeing you all again, I hope."

The next day, he said goodbye to Pete, Pedro, Hodges and Alfredo, and others. Then he and Mary set out for old John Webb's spread.

Several days later she said, as she stood stroking Shadow's neck:

"Remember, if you don't come ambling back this way soon, I'll come looking for you. That's not a threat, it's a promise."

"And a nice promise to carry with me," he replied smilingly, and rode away, to where duty called and danger and new adventure waited.

ABOUT THE AUTHOR

Bradford Scott was a pseudonym for **Leslie Scott** who was born in Lewisburg, West Virginia. During the Great War, he joined the French Foreign Legion and spent four years in the trenches. In the 1920s he worked as a mining engineer and bridge builder in the western American states and in China before settling in New York. A barroom discussion in 1934 with Leo Margulies, who was managing editor for Standard Magazines, prompted Scott to try writing fiction. He went on to create two of the most notable series characters in Western pulp magazines. In 1936, Standard Magazines launched, and in *Texas Rangers,* Scott under the house name of **Jackson Cole** created Jim Hatfield, Texas Ranger, a character whose popularity was so great with readers that this magazine featuring his adventures lasted until 1958. When others eventually began contributing Jim Hatfield stories,

Scott created another Texas Ranger hero, Walt Slade, better known as *El Halcon,* the Hawk, whose exploits were regularly featured in *Thrilling Western.* In the 1950s Scott moved quickly into writing book-length adventures about both Jim Hatfield and Walt Slade in long series of original paperback Westerns. At the same time, however, Scott was also doing some of his best work in hardcover Westerns published by Arcadia House; thoughtful, well-constructed stories, with engaging characters and authentic settings and situations. Among the best of these, surely, are *Silver City* (1953), *Longhorn Empire* (1954), *The Trail Builders* (1956), and *Blood on the Rio Grande* (1959). In these hardcover Westerns, many of which have never been reprinted, Scott proved himself highly capable of writing traditional Western stories with characters who have sufficient depth to change in the course of the narrative and with a degree of authenticity and historical accuracy absent from many of his series stories.

We hope you have enjoyed this Large Print book. Other Thorndike, Wheeler, Kennebec, and Chivers Press Large Print books are available at your library or directly from the publishers.

For information about current and upcoming titles, please call or write, without obligation, to:

Publisher
Thorndike Press
295 Kennedy Memorial Drive
Waterville, ME 04901
Tel. (800) 223-1244

or visit our Web site at:

http://gale.cengage.com/thorndike

OR

Chivers Large Print
published by BBC Audiobooks Ltd
St James House, The Square
Lower Bristol Road
Bath BA2 3SB
England
Tel. +44(0) 800 136919
email: bbcaudiobooks@bbc.co.uk
www.bbcaudiobooks.co.uk

All our Large Print titles are designed for easy reading, and all our books are made to last.